the CHRONOKEY

Death in Time

carmel morris

GRYPHON
CHESS
PUBLISHERS

Copyright 2012, Gryphon Chess Publishers

First published by Gryphon Chess Publishers 2012.

ISBN: 978-0-9873447-0-0

Cover design: Gryphon Chess

Illustrations: Donald Harris Jr.

Editor: Jim Parsons

Line sketches: Carmel Morris

Typeset in Palatino Linotype 11pt

This edition printed in the United States of America

10 9 8 7 6 5 4 3 2 1

The right of Carmel Morris to be identified as the author has been asserted in accordance with the Copyright, Designs and Patents Act, 1988

National Library of Australia CiP entry - Morris, Carmel, date-
The Chronokey: Death in Time (pbk.)

Young adult fantasy/science fiction

A823.4

For my husband, for James and Jane, for Stephanie and Tara who died so young, those who have passed on in my life in the space of four years. And for those of you I know who have suffered abuse at the hands of others who pretend to be good – you will never be forgotten.

Contents

1: Nearly Departed

The pain shot through his head, ringing out like a bullet blast that echoed into the distance. The dream began to break but Zane still felt drawn to it, a flash and rumble of orange clouds, trees igniting to flames and shattered glass splintering the air.

The burning sky dissolved to more immediacy as he grasped the fading fragments with his mind and now a screeching station wagon kicked up dust on the driveway, a neighbor's dog incessantly barking in the background. Some kind of flashlight aimed his way and his own dog, Mitch, a Jack Russell terrier, barked in response, Mitch's wide brown eyes staring past him with a mix of mad excitement and frowned desperation. The image of Mitch stayed a moment before it too slipped away to darkness.

Zane's eyelids felt glued together as he tried to wrench them open against the weight of sleep. He felt a chill from underneath and wondered why everything was so dark. He struggled to see and, wondering what time it was, he probed for his bedside clock but it was not there.

He groaned, his muffled voice returning with resonance and he wondered if half of him was still clasping onto that dream. He remembered the only other time he was conscious of being in the middle of a dream and it was an uncanny, unsettling feeling. But this could no longer be a dream as the blankness around him now felt curiously real.

A soft light filtered into his immediate surroundings though he couldn't figure where it came from. Through cloudy eyes, something took shape before him, walls perhaps and a ceiling though focus was difficult. A biting smell of wood varnish caused his nostrils to twitch and for a moment he thought the tip of his nose was motionless, paralyzed in the lacquered air.

Something thudded above him.

The sound was soft and muffled and repeated every five seconds or so. Zane listened more intently and heard faint scraping sounds between the thuds. Guessing the sound came from outside, he opened one eye a little further, expecting the glue of sleep to intrude.

Walls seemed distant but felt close; his focus was shifting and difficult to settle. This is a small room of some kind, he concluded. A prank maybe, he thought, nodding in agreement that Higgins and his buddies must have carried out their threat, knocked him out and thrown him into the local dumpster, slamming the lid tight.

"Well, he did it to Alfred," Zane mumbled in the chilly air, "So why can't I stinkin' remember? Anyway, the smell's all wrong ... where's the trash?"

An image flashed before his mind's eye of his hand latching onto Mitch's kicking leg, the paws slipping through his grip. Zane shuddered from the image and blinked hard, forcing his eyes to focus on his surroundings. The thudding stopped for a moment and he caught faint voices. Some were familiar.

The thudding then returned, much closer this time. It felt like his heart. He reached to clasp his chest and his hand sunk into his body. He felt his heart pounding but the feeling was odd, like an empty thrashing in the air. He examined his legs and arms and knew then that the soft light around him came from within him, from his own body. But his body refused to move except for the glowing haze that surrounded it. He watched the juddering image of his hand as he waved it in the air. He wiggled his toes and could feel the sensation. He swayed his feet from left to right and saw the gleaming outline of his shoes moving as expected. A shiver rippled up his spine when he noticed another pair of shoes. They didn't move at all. They remained glossy and motionless, a well-polished pair he hated wearing.

The shoes that moved were not the same. He looked hard and picked out the pair of cheap, comfortable trainers he always wore about the place, the shoes Mom threatened to throw away. Still in a dream, he thought, must be a dream.

"A dream," he whispered slowly.

Before he could even attempt to understand this condition another thud came from above. He squeezed his eyelids tight, probing the fleeting memories and trying to latch onto a scene; he imagined he had his hand on a remote control, trying to slow down, if not freeze, the simultaneous fast forwarding and rewinding of memories now dashing before him. But the memories slipped in and out through a blur of fading colors that dissolved to nothing.

He opened his eyes slowly and waved his shimmering hand in the half-light, imagining himself watching an old, poorly tuned analog television set that shifted and ghosted, like the one Granddad has.

"Gh-ghost..." The words stammered through his trembling lips and he swallowed hard, feeling a bulge in his throat that refused to clear.

"Can't be... I... I f-feel alive." He forced the words over rising fear.

Thud...

"Mom!" he yelled to the stillness.

Desperation now swelled from within. No voices returned and for a moment he wondered if his mother and family and friends were a million miles away.

"Just where the stink am I?"

Thud...

A rupturing fear seemed to gurgle up from deep inside as Zane stretched his eyes open a little further. He felt amazed at how he could see anything in such poor light. The surrounding walls now felt closer, the thudding sound outside a little softer. Something was smothering, something outside that felt thickening and embracing.

And then the words spilled from his mouth before he had time to grasp their impact. Slowly but harshly in the darkness he said, "This room's a coffin, and I'm stinkin' dead!"

2: Goodbyes

He felt like he was juddering all over with shock and now he could see the outline of his murky shape brighten in the darkness.

He shifted his focus to close quarters and he could now clearly make out the walls of his enclosure, a harsh unfinished pine slapped in stain.

"Can't be," he whispered heavily, "It don't feel right."

He gazed around the walls of his enclosure.

"If Mom didn't have much money, why bury me? Why not burn me? How'd I die anyway? So cold in here... where's the tunnel of light? Where's heaven or," he gulped, "that other stinkin' place?"

A swelling of emotion erupted through the fear and shock. Something now clouded his vision and he blinked. He knew then he was crying and he knew he could blink but just how baffled him. He bit his lip and actually felt numbness. He blinked several times to clear the foggy streams of what he thought could be tears in his eyes.

Zane examined the walls of his coffin and touched the rough wood with a finger that glowed softly, appeared transparent but had the color and depth to look almost normal. He pressed against the coffin wall with his finger and it throbbed before penetrating the wood.

"Wow!" he said, forcing a chuckle. "Weird death." He looked more intently at how his finger melded into the wood. Instantly, the wood faded, became smoky and colorless. Zane stared at the strange blend of finger and wood and soon realized that he could see past it to the dirt outside and the rocks and twigs beyond.

He focused his eyes, then unfocussed, the surrounding wood and soil shifting in transparent folds of dim light. Layers appeared to strip away the more he concentrated, as if his eyes were burning through the ground. He relaxed his eyes and the layers of rock and soil weaved back over themselves quickly.

He looked above at his closer surroundings. Worms coiled through the soft fresh soil, churned by the spade above. Zane looked further upwards and concentrated his vision through the soil to fresh flowers, the light suddenly cascading down and drowning his eyes for a moment.

And then he saw them.

Mom stood in the bracing air looking down into space, perhaps another place in her mind, perhaps a peaceful place for Zane to rest. The wind swept past her. She stood unmoved except for the sails of her long dusky hair, while others remained close and comforted her. The sky beyond was a deep autumn blue that sparkled and shifted with speckled gray streaks of unusual, elongated clouds.

Zane breathed deeply, the glow of what he thought was a kind of spiritual exhalation misted the air, and he felt relieved that some friends from class showed up. He tried to think back to the moment of his death. He probed hard into a memory that was blinded by some kind of impact.

"All I can see is Mitch. Why Mitch? It's gotta come back to me..."

He felt another swelling tear emerge, glistening and blocking his vision momentarily. He touched the corner of his eye and the tear was wet. He could see the droplet and feel it slide past his finger to fall and tap the wooden floor of the coffin where it dissolved to nothing. He couldn't understand why he didn't sink into the ground below him like his teardrop just did and a sudden panging for knowledge filled him as he regretted the hours of daydreaming in class – but what would a teacher know about death? What would anyone alive know?

For a brief moment his mother's eyes met his. He felt a swelling sadness at the back of his eyes, a sorrow that could never be resolved. He knew she couldn't see him and it was just dumb luck he could look straight into her eyes. His sister Jennifer pulled at her overcoat and Mom gave her a warm embrace but fixed her gaze upon the grave before her. Neither cried but Zane knew they would sooner or later. Maybe when they get home to an empty house, or at dinner time, Mom will break into tears. That's what she did when Dad left.

That's what she's probably already done over me, he concluded.

And of course Dad didn't show up. Why should he? Zane tried to picture him but it was cloudy and difficult and his sadness broke the images, until an instant need for him caused the scene with the station wagon to fill his mind for a moment. The dust, a quick getaway. Zane could never figure why such a stranger to him would return, but from a distance take flight. And now Dad was just a stubbly-faced, dying memory from a dead son.

Zane suddenly chuckled, a sick despondent chuckle which he promptly choked upon and he wondered if his father knew he was dead.

"Mom, you always said I grew up fast when he left," Zane mumbled. "Jen, you'll have to take over now."

Zane pushed the thoughts aside and looked beyond his grave to his family. "Ah, Jake Numan, there you are, pal, companion troublemaker. How will those teachers cope with one nuisance down? You'll have to be on your guard from now on. Look at you standing there, glum and fidgety in your ill-fitting uniform. Almost didn't recognize ya, buddy, that parachute of a shirt tucked in and your tie straight and this time not used as a replacement belt to hold up your baggy turd-catching trousers. Wonder if you'll ever grow out of that skin and bones body?"

He saw somebody standing behind Jake, his head lifting momentarily.

"Yes!" Zane said loudly with delight. "Alfred, good on ya for coming. They all think you're a dweeb but I know you're the best. You know more than anyone."

Alfred stood in the distance, hesitant to approach Zane's grave, his face sullied by crying.

"It's okay, buddy," Zane said loudly. "Guys can cry. You came and glad no bullies followed you this time. Courage, my freckly dweeb friend."

Jake took Jennifer's hand and held it gently, then embraced her and Mom.

17

And then it hit Zane with a pounding realization. They will all grow up, get jobs, get married and get old.

"And I can't change now, not ever I guess."

He sank back and rested hands behind head; he could actually feel his fingers through his thick matted hair.

"So, if this is death, where are all the other stinkin' dead folk?"

His voice bounded off the coffin wood and resonated through his head. "Heaven? Hell?" He raised his voice. "Hello?" He sighed and mumbled, "Don't see any paths to either place, just mortals wandering around above me, and now they're leaving."

Jake kicked the loose clumps of soil nearby until his mother took his arm and led him away. Mom and Jennifer were the last two to stay. They turned slowly and headed for the car. Zane wanted to cry out loud and thought he heard himself do just that, but of course he knew they wouldn't turn to hear him. If only he could see them again. He panged with sudden loss as he struggled in his coffin, feeling nailed to his remains. Now the people were going.

"This sure is stinkin' Hell," he cursed. "I can't even break free to follow them."

He looked away for a moment and then glanced up to notice Jake bent over his grave, peering down at him with a perplexed, almost angry look on his pimply face. Zane felt eerie seeing someone looking in his direction but unable to notice his return gaze.

"So you had to go and die on me, yeah?" Jake bellowed, flicking his sandy hair away from his eyes. "Who's gonna stand up to my dad now? I'm going to miss you, mate, miss your silly geek face, that stupid laser pointer of yours and those water bombs, you dead asshole. Push some flowers so I know you're down there doing somethin'."

A hand grabbed Jake's arm, his mother pulling him to leave. He shook free until she took his hand and gently tugged him away.

Zane spotted a glint in his left eye. Jake never cries, never.

Jake's mother looked back over her shoulder, her face flat, devoid of emotion; only a tinge of blue jutted under her left eye and that wasn't a tear stain. It looked more like a new bruise.

Zane had to look away. Life would go on for them, no matter how brutal. He tried to focus on something else. He glanced around the coffin, the soil outside, the grass above and the cars in the distance all circling away. He began to feel uncomfortable now that everyone had left.

"Can't get over this see-through-matter thing," he muttered. "I can burn my eyes through the stuff, a bit like x-ray vision." He looked harder through the soil to his right.

A hollow pair of eyes stared straight back at him, leering through the dirt beyond. Zane shrieked, jolting backwards; he expected a skeletal arm to lunge through the dirt and into his coffin, groping for his neck. But nothing sank through his coffin wall and he fell back with relief and released a heavy sigh, regretting all those horror videos he had watched with Jake and Alfred.

He carefully aimed his eyes back through the dirt, just to punish himself with one more look at the skeleton in the next grave.

"Err…"

Zane could see it more clearly now. From a rotted coffin a sunken hairy skull smirked back at him in stony silence. Zane shivered and thought the sensation was like static electricity from a woolen pullover.

"All this feeling," he gasped. "Can't believe it but I *do* feel; I actually have feelings. So why do I feel stuck to this dead body? Maybe the more I rot, the more I can detach myself – but that'll take time, I guess."

The sensation then rippled down his ghostly form, a tickle of electricity that caused him to suddenly shake violently.

"Wicked," he breathed, "I can move after all..."

"Of course you can move," a sharp hollow voice bellowed from above. "You're dead, Zane, you dead dummy!"

"AH!" Zane shrieked again.

He stared through the dirt at the motionless skull. Nothing moved there, except a worm coiling into its broken nostril. He tried to scope his eyes through the dirt beyond his adjacent graves but he could see nothing and yet, somewhere out there, someone had spoken his name.

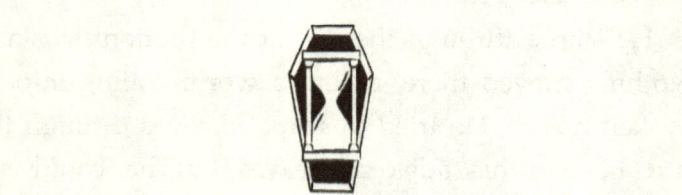

3: Angela

"Hey... Zany dude..."

"Wh – who said that?"

There was no reply. That voice was clear and loud and it had addressed him and it sounded like it was right beside him, but it had a neutral tone and he wasn't sure if it came from a man or woman. Zane tried to figure how sound worked in the afterlife but dismissed the thought as too complicated.

"Where are you?" he yelled again.

"Up here, dummy," the voice cackled. "Oh sorry … Zany."

"How'd you know my name?"

"On your stone, stupid," replied the voice, laughing. "Turned in your grave yet? Bet you hadn't thought about that expression before."

"Now I'm getting miffed," Zane grumbled. And then he suddenly wondered how his headstone would be there so quickly after he died and he thought of the expense this would have cost his mother And then he remembered what Jake said about his uncle's funeral, how laser stone engraving is getting more common and cheaper now; perhaps that's what happened.

Sadness returned for a moment and he pushed it aside, shifting his focus to breaking free. His ghostly shaking now vibrated to a fast electric rhythm, shimmering intensely while his body still felt like it was glued to the wood underneath.

And then he felt the sensation of slowly tearing away from his corpse.

"How's that ephemeral carcass doing, Zane?" the voice above boomed, "Still holding you back?"

"I feel like I'm gaffer taped," Zane said as he struggled to break free.

He caught a faint giggle and for a moment thought he could pick out a girl's voice. Squinting hard, he began to make out the orb-like shape of something hovering above his grave, wheeling around his gleaming new headstone, diving towards him and then sweeping up to the trees above before coming back to a hover over him again.

"It'll take you time," the voice said with a laugh. "But you have all the time in the universe."

"What do you know about it?" Zane cried. "Wait till I get outa here…"

He sprung upright, his head protruding through the coffin lid into the soil above. He imagined his form would appear blurry and not well-defined as he lifted up his glowing arms, furry clouds of light like a swollen cottony rag doll, all glimmering and rough around the edges. He looked up through the soil and beyond the grave, then back at his own glowing arms. "Must be some kind of focus thing," he mumbled.

"That's right," the voice bantered. "Focus, you dead dummy, focus..."

Zane tried to wrench further from his corpse and the more he tried, the more he could see his own true shape, focusing on what he should normally look like. He wondered about that thing above waiting for him to leave this grave. Kind of scary in a way, he thought, but at least something out there could see and speak to him.

"Hurry up," cried the voice above.

"Well, I'm dying to get outa here," Zane yelled back.

"Very good," the voice laughed. "But it'll take you a bit of time. If you were cremated it may have been different."

"Oh yeah?" He struggled again. He looked back down at his doughy body, his dead face, eyes closed and motionless but seemingly determined to hold onto him. His legs felt clasped and he struggled more vigorously. And then he noticed his glowing spirit

25

brighten. He tingled all over and the charge increased throughout his being as if someone had given him a jolt of electricity.

"Gonna break free from this stinkin' body," Zane gasped under his breath.

"Not stinking yet, but soon will be," the voice teased.

Zane gritted what felt like his teeth, the frustration channeling through him with increasing strength and determination and he began to wonder where this energy was coming from.

And then the tingling sensation instantly dispersed.

Zane suddenly felt buoyant and sensed he was breathing deeply with relief, though how he dared not contemplate. He rose up slowly through the soil, past marble and flowers.

This is so weird but I don't care, he thought excitedly. I just want to see that annoying spirit above me. "Hey you," he yelled. "I gotta stinkin' bone to pick with you!"

"Hah-hah, you got a few back there, bone head," the voice above laughed. "C'mon then, I'm waiting." The hovering clouded light ascended to the tree tops above.

"I must get *out* of here," Zane said under breath. "Are you a spirit like me?"

With a haughty laugh, the voice replied, "Gross... Who'd wanna be like you?"

That did it. Zane no longer felt any recognizable fear, just determination and anger. "You don't have to be rude about it," he yelled. He glanced down, and for a moment fear gripped him again for now he floated some twenty feet above the ground.

"You're not used to this, are you, Zany?"

"Don't call me that!"

Zane spotted the glow that was his tormenter slip behind a dense tree. He approached it cautiously – though how he moved through the air, he had no idea.

He focused on his anger to smother any fear that could rise at any moment; he wondered what this bully spirit could really do to him now that he was dead. He was glad the uncanny feeling of nothing underfoot had settled somewhat as he carefully feathered his form over the many headstones below.

He squinted to see through the tree, just as he had done to peer through the soil above his grave. The leaves swayed in the breeze, making it difficult to focus through it. He looked around the cemetery and it was then he noticed the strangeness in the air. The outside world looked the same, though somewhat hazy, the gray streaky clouds he noticed earlier appeared as a sort of pollution but he knew it wasn't that, more like clumpy vapors in the form of cloudy tubes swirling around, some quite low, meandering through the lush grounds. The misty snake-like trails intertwined with each other but did not seem to blend. Some were lighter than others though they were all gray, just many shades of it.

"Only the dead can see the funnels," said the voice, shooting past him in a half-second gust of wind.

"Who are you?" Zane demanded.

"Another ghost, stupid," the voice replied. "Dead like you, sort of. Hey, seen any demons?"

"Demons?"

"Yeah – and devils, ghouls and all manner of beastly things. If you ain't in Heaven, then they'll *get* you."

Zane scanned the grounds in a sudden return of panic. "Where?"

"They come out when you're not looking and—" the voice broke into reeling laughter. "Silly boy!"

"Thanks," Zane said sullenly. "Thanks for the joke. There aren't any, are there?"

The spirit remained silent.

"So you're a ghost then," Zane asked.

"Of course," the voice replied in an almost pompous tone.

The spirit approached him slowly from behind another tree. Zane could barely make out its form, just as he had trouble making out his own ghostly shape. Then he spotted a milky grin emerging from the shapeless being, a straight row of teeth glinting in the light.

"What sort of ghost?" he asked. "How old?"

"Just turned sixteen and I know you're younger," the spirit replied flatly.

Zane searched for any kind of thing to say that would seem normal, just to stave off the unsettling feeling of this strange visitor. "Wow! Almost a whole two years older. You probably had a good idea of what you wanted to do with your life then. Mom always hassled about what I wanted to do with my life. Didn't know then and now I guess I'll never know."

"Guess you'll never know."

The voice was softer that time and didn't seem as hostile; Zane relaxed a little. He watched the vapors or funnels as his host called them. They swirled all around them, but not too close which deep down, for some reason, made him feel more at ease. "So what happens now?"

"Well," the spirit began, "I could make a judgment."

"A judgment..." Zane gulped. "Judgment Day?"

"Oh no," the spirit said through a chuckle, "Let's just say I could guess."

"Guess at what?" he asked as he looked down to his grave. Some pigeons were pulling at the flowers around his headstone. "If I'm here I'm probably lost without destiny," Zane said glumly.

"Oh, you're wrong, you silly sad thing," said the ghost in a slight mocking tone. "Life begins after death."

"Yeah, right," Zane scoffed. "I've heard that before from a couple of stinkin' jerks in suits at our front door. They kept coming back; must've felt sorry for us. They talked about good and evil and if you do this or that you'll burn in hell. My Dad, when he was around, would tell them to beat it, because he didn't like blackmail or spiritual bribes. He didn't like being threatened by anyone, even God."

"My, you're an angry thing," the host ghost replied.

Zane looked away.

A silence passed while Zane's hovering host swooped down upon the pigeons pulling at his flowers. They seemed to notice the strange spirit – how Zane didn't know. They fluttered in a frenzy of feathers as if something had just freaked them and then flew off in separate directions.

"How'd you do that?" Zane asked.

The spirit ignored him. "Good and evil are confusing, just like the shades of those funnels," it said, pointing a shimmery arm. "Nothing is black and white."

Zane watched the strange vapors swirl across the horizon as light and dark mists writhing together like two snakes having sex like the two pythons Jake kept last year had done. And although they were hazy, they didn't seem to meld together.

The spirit pointed a furry arm of glistening light. "See that gardener over there by the big oak tree."

"What about him?"

"Concentrate, dummy," the voice said sternly.

Zane focused hard and made out a pale gray aura surrounding the gardener whose entire body emitted a gray light. "He's got what looks like a force field about him," Zane said slowly.

"Not quite a force field, more like an aura. But auras and force fields are similar, so my dad said. All living things have one. When a funnel gets really close to a living being, you can see the aura around that being."

"So this aura is the same as personal space or something?"

"Maybe."

"Well what then?"

"I've heard that people, everyone, absorb certain amounts of the strange energy from the funnels that come and go, that the funnels contain essences of good and evil and the aura is the extension of our bodies – us."

"Seriously?" Zane laughed. "More like spectrums of light that living folk can't see, or some kind of radiation that cannot be seen by human eye or detected by instruments."

"Why analyze it in living terms? Dad used to do that. He worked with magnetic fields and something he joked about called dense Kirlian energy, which is not the same as regular coronal discharging but is contained in a field, not that I understand it. We could have something similar. He said you could see regular transpiring energy by taking special photos. It's energy shaped by life. But alive you wouldn't know it's there, except maybe when you get the creepy feeling your personal space is invaded by someone moving close to you, like a stranger. But it's more than that."

"Right," Zane said flatly.

The spirit hovered away from him, and then swooped back up to his face, causing Zane to feel uncomfortable, as if his own personal space was invaded. "You seem to doubt everything, Zane."

"Goes with the family tree, I suppose," Zane said glumly.

The spirit was so close now Zane could make out the shape of it, the dark eyes of a color he could not determine, small upturned nose and a smallish rounded face – a girl's face framed in a rusty-colored bob with a long, uncertain fringe.

"I've been dead a little bit longer than you, Zane, so I have more experience. And I could move straight away after I died, maybe because my body was cremated. Nothing to hold on to me, I could move around more quickly without being tied to a rotting corpse."

"But I'm up here with you now," Zane said stubbornly. He looked away from her surprised face and huffed. "You've just cheated the carbon cycle. Worms and a moist weedy place to rest is all I need now, I guess. What else is there?"

"Rest?" she laughed. "The young don't rest."

"Why not?"

"Because they *don't*," she said quickly.

Zane wondered if she simply didn't have the answer. He gazed across the rolling lawns of the cemetery. Headstones were nicely spaced apart with lots of open grounds. It must have cost Mom a bomb to put me here, he thought. A breeze picked up in the autumn afternoon. Their two glows gave no response to the wind. Zane made out his host's face again, deep colorless eyes slowly turning to a greenish-brown, strands of her rusty hair lifting and lowering as she feathered through the air.

"Do you have a name?" he asked.

"Of course, dummy."

"And?"

She hesitated. "Angela... Angela Moore."

Zane watched her hazy aura float up and down over his grave. He could now make out her shape, skinny and helpless-looking, and he felt a little more comfortable seeing her this way instead of seeing a threatening orb of light.

"How'd you..." he gestured, slitting his neck with his finger, "you-know..."

She ignored him but for a slight, almost disinterested smile. Her skinny shape appeared to sway in the breeze now but Zane knew the wind wasn't causing it. He couldn't stop staring at her, another ghost like him.

"It's weird..." he said slowly. "Looking at you is like looking at one of those hidden 3D images."

"Only we're in another dimension altogether," she said approaching him, "and you can see me more clearly if *I* concentrate on my appearance. You must concentrate too. The weird thing is, though, when I travel, my form melts into a ball of cloud, like it's reshaping for speed or something."

"Like a slogger?" Zane laughed.

"What's that?"

"A spit ball."

"Gross. You are such low income."

"Sorry. Just trying to see if you'd react."

"Sure," she huffed. "I was brought up better than you, it seems."

"Whatever you say, your highness," Zane said tersely.

Her voice went soft. "Sorry. I didn't mean that. It's been so lonely out here. It's nice to finally catch up with another ghost again, even you."

"Thanks..." Zane said cautiously, "I think..." With sudden nervousness he asked, "Can you see me well enough?" He hoped she wouldn't see the freckles which he knew were still there at the tip of his nose and below his eyes in a fuzzy arc of random dots.

"Yes," she said flatly, "a black-haired scruffy geek city boy with big blue eyes that look like spotlights at a rave party. You could be the annoying younger brother I never had and you need a haircut. Bit late now. And do up your shoelaces." She said.

"I did!" he protested. "They keep untying themselves."

Her spirit suddenly spun away, sweeping back to complete a huge circle spanning several graves. "We must move on —"

"Wait!" He began to feel uncomfortable. He looked around the graveyard and figured the graves of others must be empty, as no other ghost had greeted him. They must have gone somewhere, he guessed, but where?

"You must come with me," she urged. "Someone's gotta break you into death and I'm the only one around here."

"I want to see Mom again."

"Not now, we must *go*," she stressed. "Dumpster Man says we must move on or be eaten."

Zane felt that fear return. "Eaten? Eaten by what? Not those demons you mentioned?"

"No, silly," her voice began to quaver, "More creepy than demons and I haven't been able to find him again to find out why they come."

"What are they? Who's this Dumpster Man?"

She hesitated. "Someone... someone I ran into after my death, someone weird who likes junk."

"Alive?" Zane asked. "You mean someone alive who can see you?"

Angela looked behind and panicked and Zane spotted it too. A dark gray funnel hovered towards them. Zane could feel his hazy heart pounding more rapidly and it felt solid as if he was alive and active like jogging or something and he wondered how on earth the sensation of being alive in a ghostly form worked.

"Wrong one," she said quickly. She grabbed Zane's hand and yanked him up and through the tree tops, away from the dark funnel. "You've gotta be able to move faster, Zane, or you won't know where you are in an instant."

"Eh?" Zane's hand tingled from her touch as they sailed through the leaves.

"Okay," she panted, "We're safe for now. Don't see anything else bad."

That's spooky, Zane thought as he looked at his strange host. He wondered how she could pull on his spirit and make him move with her, and she was panting, as if she was gasping for air too. He felt his own sensation of breathing, even though logically ghosts shouldn't need to breathe air. He thought it strange how the dead act like they're still alive.

She looked at him oddly. "Okay?"

"Fine, I think."

"Look Zane, you've gotta come with me where I go, at least for now," she said. "Got to break you into death."

"Uh-huh," he said lightly.

She scanned the sky with nervous eyes and took his arm again.

A soft tingle ran up what he felt was his spine.

"You can move faster, Zane," she said. "Till now you've been, well, dead slow. All you have to do is to concentrate on moving easily in your desired direction."

Only one way to find out, Zane thought. He focused his eyes on the giant spruce tree nearby and imagined he wanted to fly to it. Instantly he swept through the air as if the air itself was not there to slow him down or blow his hair away from his face. There was no resistance, like a spiritual vacuum or perhaps being flung out in space.

"Wow, this is like... I don't know what!" He dove down through the trees and zoomed around the graveyard. "Woo, watch me fly..."

"Don't be over-confident," Angela warned as she caught up with him. "Even death has some surprises."

"Sur-prises?" he asked slowly.

"Well, why should I tell you?" she sneered. "Wouldn't be a surprise."

"That sort of teasing went out when my cousin turned five," Zane said defiantly. He looked at his strange new friend, a funny mix of maturity and childlike mannerisms. She's not that much older than me, he thought.

"There's a lot you have to learn, Zane," she said coldly.

Zane folded his shimmering arms. "A lot we both have to learn, I reckon. You just got a head start. I'll cope. Had to when my stinkin' Dad took off and had to support Mom and all that. Bit of a bummer being dead now. I wanted so much to find out why that son of a bitch old man bastard stink breath took off the way he did."

"Ooh, such temper," she said. "What did he do... for a job?"

"Some stinkin' insurance broker or something like that, I think. Not sure."

"You don't know what your father did?"

"It was always different," Zane protested. "He always had different jobs. Mom said he was shiftless, whatever that meant, like he couldn't get his life in gear and he didn't know what he wanted to do. Guess

I could relate to that 'cause I got no idea what I want to do either."

"Too late now," Angela said lightly.

"Huh?"

"You're a dead duck, Zane," she said with a sneer, "*stinking* dead as you say. Dead-dead-dead-deady-dead!"

"Don't remind me," he mumbled, gazing across the cemetery. "I've only just come out of the ground, you know."

Angela sprang around the giant spruce, spinning her way down to the trunk, laughing. "Poor widdle Zane, rotting away for the worms and the ghouls, such a forlorn sad little ghosty."

"Hey, cool it!"

And then her puffed-up face, twisted smile and curious right eyelid flicking oddly caused him to turn away.

"I get the message," he said flatly.

"You have to get used to your new situation," she said quietly, looking up at the sky. The sun was setting now and a few stars began to pierce the fading blue. "We can explore this afterlife. Perhaps we'll find out why—" She turned away quickly.

"What?"

She paused. Her voice had quivered a little, though Zane felt it was more from loneliness than fear. He wondered who the hell she was, anyway, why she had come to his grave and not others. Perhaps, he mused with caution, she knew more about him than he knew about himself.

He suddenly felt the urge to fly away from here, but felt a conflicting urge to stay and find out more, because Heaven or Hell hadn't called him, if they ever existed at all, and here he was all conscious in the afterlife.

"Which grave are you from?" he asked.

"Not here," she said with a solemn look on her face. She turned slowly, the expression on her face creasing with concern. "Fact is, Zane, we were both cut off early from the living world." She quickly glanced behind her. "And there's something I haven't told you."

Zane winced at the thought of another nasty surprise.

"Zane," Angela said slowly, "The way we travel, to see new places, we have a sort of random travel arrangement. I've wandered far and fell upon you because a funnel swept me here."

"Now I'm confused – a funnel? Aren't we supposed to stay away from them?"

"I didn't say that. Funnels are like travel tubes or subways of the afterlife, or slinkies that stretch the skies; the trip is sometimes long but often short, as if the slinky has contracted or something. Some funnels are darker than others and I prefer to travel in the lighter ones, as the destination is not so unpleasant. Sometimes they change, go lighter or darker, and I don't like that, but I cannot ignore the darker ones, just the really black ones. I'm scared of those."

"Why?"

"You don't want to know," she said flatly. "Once, where I landed was bad, very bad."

"Yet you'll put up with some unpleasantness, go into a dark gray one?" he asked, getting more curious.

"I'm hoping one day to find out what happened to my Dad. There wasn't a trace of him in the debris. I thought the blast may have gotten him but he can't be found, alive or dead; that is, I haven't run into him since I died. And the Dumpster Man can't or won't tell me. I'm not sure but I know he knows heaps."

"Blast?"

"So terrible," she said gloomily, her head tilting with sudden sadness. "Dad's factory and lab, some confidential experiment gone wrong. So much of the place had been blown to nothing. No one knows if it was an accident or sabotage."

Zane stared at her in disbelief. He couldn't think of a worse way to go.

Angela hovered to his side and Zane could tell her glow felt kind of warm, which seemed to make the surrounding air feel colder.

"At least your dad didn't want to leave you," he said glumly.

Her frosty hand tapped his before retracting with a sensation of static electricity, mixed with uncertainty he could see in her eyes. She hesitantly took his hand and clasped it and both of them instantly warmed as if covered by an invisible blanket. Her deep hazy eyes staring at him with curiosity mixed with what Zane guessed might be a subtle hint of revulsion for some reason or other – perhaps because he was 'so low income'.

"You're real... here," she said wistfully. "You're not taken. It's been a while since I've seen another ghost."

"Not taken?"

"Shhhh…" she breathed.

Zane was sure he caught her breath, and their touch, it was the strangest kind of heat or energy exchange. Maybe that's what spirits do, to sort of survive, just share their glow. He looked down at their clasp and then at her face, which had now fallen into a soft curious and almost feeble-looking gaze.

Her eyes widened. "It's here. We're part of one now. Soon we'll be carried away."

Zane hadn't realized what was happening around them until then. Their immediate surroundings became hazy as a funnel closed in, the vapors swirling around in vertical circles, closing together to make a thick cloudy-ribbed wall. Zane could now only see in two directions, behind and in front down a long winding tunnel that swayed in various disorientating angles, causing him to feel a little dizzy. He thought it could be exciting, not knowing where he was going, or where the funnel originated from in all its randomness. And how could she ever find her father? He could be at the other end of a black funnel and she may have to face that one day.

Zane gaped at the puffy gray walls of cloud, not too dark, though the shade varied as the walls became thicker. "It's like we're inside a giant slinky, or perhaps a vacuum cleaner hose," he said, "and we're a couple of clumps of fuzzy dust sucked inside."

Angela held her hand out to touch the surface of the funnel walls which padded past her. "It feels like marshmallow," she said calmly. "We're being carried, Zane. Close your eyes and relax, we're off to another place."

He gulped and hesitantly closed his eyes.

The driving winds of this strange afterlife dashed past them and through them and at the same time swept them ever forward, Zane contemplating the winds, winds not made of air yet able to propel them. He felt compelled to open at least one eye for just a moment to see how fast they were going. A shiver rippled through him, not because he was racing through the funnel at an ever-increasing speed, for he was used to speeding on his bike down steep hills and now kind of enjoyed flying through the air which no longer frightened him.

He shivered again and closed his eye quickly from a sudden dread, for this funnel had grown dark.

4: The Arrival

Zane couldn't help thinking there was intelligence behind the funnel they traversed, to change its shade the way it did and carry them off to somewhere, maybe a bad somewhere. But then he decided that was the dumbest thing he could think of.

He watched his host calmly bob over the soft cloudy cushioned floor of the funnel and knew she'd done this many times before, and he gulped, knowing he'd have to get used to this kind of traveling. Better than being eaten back there by whatever stinkin' thing, demons or hungry ghosts. He shuddered at the thought.

"You're doing well, Zane," Angela said aloud, gripping his hands tightly.

"This funnel's got darker," Zane yelled.

"We'll be fine. Just hold on; it doesn't take long... usually."

That doesn't sound confident, he thought. He hadn't realized how ragingly loud it was in the funnel now.

They sailed awkwardly, as the funnel began to thrash and coil around them, the buffeting worsening

47

with every passing bend. Zane was thrown free from Angela's grip, the funnel wall cushioning his impact but not bouncing him to the other side, and he felt relieved not to shoot right through the cottony wall altogether.

"This ride's gotten rough," Angela yelled through the whistling air. "Something's wrong."

The funnel groaned as they roared down its coiling torrent towards a flickering, distant light – an opening, Zane hoped.

And then something caused Zane to turn. A pinprick of sound twitched his ears. It was a voice deep and crusty. Someone was speaking, the voice repeating a series of words he could barely make out and he closed his eyes as the voices slowly faded to nothing.

"What the stinkin' hell was it?" he mumbled to himself.

"What?" Angela asked.

"Nah," he said. "It's in my stinkin' head."

"What is?"

"Nothing, Ange," Zane said quickly.

With a high-pitched crackling shrill they whooshed out of the funnel through a jagged hole, Zane making out a shredded section of brick and plaster that allowed them to exit to a dimly-lit room.

He opened his eyes to tattered wallpaper, the peeling layers jutting into his face and he pushed himself back from the meld, turning to gather his bearings.

They had landed in someone's bedroom. A man in a rumpled business shirt lay slumped face-down on the bed.

Angela pushed herself away from a landscape painting hanging crookedly over the bed, her ghost appearing as if glued to it from the impact of arrival. She recoiled with ease and smiled hesitantly.

"Wow," Zane breathed.

"That was a ghastly ride," she said with a tone of surprise, "and a rough exit. It's not normally like that. Look at that wall where we came through," she said, pointing. "All singed, like the funnel had burned a hole. But they're not supposed to do that... maybe it was 'cause there were two of us riding in it?"

"Maybe," Zane panted. "But the wall's still there; it's just got a more transparent hole in it, like the wallpaper and bricks are still there but you can see through them more easily without really trying. It took more effort to see through stuff when I was in my coffin."

"Strange, I haven't seen that before," Angela said with curious, glazed eyes. "Yes... I can partly see through the bricks without having to focus my eyes through the matter. Normally a funnel exit leaves no trace, not even for a ghost to see."

Zane shrugged. "Stinkin' weird alright. Anyways, that funnel was fierce. Hope they're not all like that."

"No, they're not," she said flatly, narrowing her eyes as she scanned the room.

"This place's familiar," Zane said, his eyes bulging slowly with gathering surprise. He peered through the half-open door down the hallway and recognized the paintings on the walls. "Yeah... it's Jake's house, my friend Jake. Wow, we haven't traveled very far... still near Century City. And that must be Mister Numan," he said as he looked at the face-down form on the bed, "Jake's stinkin' dad."

"Why's everything stinking to you?"

Zane suddenly felt the urge to hide behind a chair or sneak out without being seen. He dropped to the carpet and carefully tiptoed past the snoring Mister Numan sprawled awkwardly on the unmade bed.

"No one can see you," Angela said quickly. "We're dead, remember?"

"Didn't those pigeons at my grave see you?"

"They felt something perhaps, that's all," she said flatly.

"This place feels strange," he said cautiously.

"How could it? You've been here before and no one can see you," Angela said firmly. "Think of yourself as a fly on the wall."

Zane smirked at that remark. "Even flies can be seen. I wonder—"

"Come and see..."

The words wafted through his ear drums, rumbling in subtle tones until finally fading away to a whisper.

"Did you hear that?"

"What?"

"Someone speaking."

With an almost mocking look on her face, Angela flicked aside her hair and cocked her ear to the air. "I hear nothing."

"Well, I hear a weird voice... and strange words." He looked behind, staring at the wall from where they emerged.

"Who's speaking?"

The words rumbled louder and he could now make out a haughty voice, perhaps of an adult, repeating a verse over and over. Zane swung about the room, trying to pinpoint the sound.

Angela folded her arms impatiently, eyeing Mister Numan who remained motionless on the bed. She twirled her finger through her rusty hair, her face turning sour. "You've gone bananas, Zane," she said slowly, with a look of slight surprise on her face.

Zane looked down to the floor. A cockroach scuttled under the bed. He crouched down, his lanky legs folding like a frog as he burned his finger into the filthy, cigarette-trodden carpet.

"What are you doing?" she asked in a shrill tone.

"...*earthly traps*..." the voice crackled louder from below the floor, the words resonating up his arm and into his mind with a final grating itch behind his eyes.

Zane shrunk back, his face more pallid than its ghostly norm. He glanced at Angela's infuriated eyes and stood up, forcing a haphazard half-smile. Jake's house is a single story, he mused. Nothing's below this floor, not even a basement.

But the words persisted, rolling together in a gruff, sandpapery sound that ruptured through his being before finally fading into a soft rumble...

"Come and see, those who are free,
Yet caught in earthly traps,
Truth unwinds from snaky binds,
Evil coils up then attacks."

In a stupefied daze, Zane fell back through a wall into the brick cavity of the house. The voice finally dissolved and he slowly opened his eyes to spy up the shaft of the double-brick wall.

Angela's head poked through it.

"Ah!" Zane shrieked.

"Shush, Zane. Here." She held out her arm for him to grab. "You're still not used to poking through matter, are you?"

"Guess not. And I'm still not used to your tingling touch."

"We're the same," she said. "But this stuff is different. Just think of your soul seeping through solid matter like honey through a sieve. It's easy when you get the knack of it. Soon the honey becomes water and floating through walls and the like is easy."

"But I fell through it like it wasn't there!" Zane protested.

"You weren't thinking about it then; when you think too hard, it's difficult. But back at your grave you were so annoyed at me you had to get out and you weren't thinking how you did it."

"Okay, okay," Zane said quietly. "I'll get the hang of this. Guess I'm not used to traveling in funnels with spirits or dead things or strange voices."

He looked around the filthy room and cupped his ear to the air, finally releasing a sigh. "It's gone."

"Just what's going on with you?" she demanded.

"I don't know. That stinkin' voice, you didn't hear it did you," he said glumly.

She barked with laughter. "You are indeed a funny one."

Maybe she's right, he thought. And why should I care? It's just a voice. Mister Numan certainly didn't hear it. "I wonder," he started, "if that voice came from another dimension via another funnel, or followed us here in our funnel."

"Forget the voice," Angela snapped.

"Well, there must be a reason for it."

"Do you have to put a purpose to everything, Zane?" She folded her arms again, eyeing him carefully.

Zane stood confused, his bright blue eyes sharp and penetrating under that short scrappy fringe, eyes not quite knowing what to look for.

Angela watched him wave his long, skinny arm through the bedside table and saw his freckly face light up with small delight. She suddenly asked, "I wonder if you would have grown up to be quite tall and lanky or filled out."

"What?"

"Never mind," she said quickly.

Zane groaned. "I can't wait for a funnel to come and take us away from here. This place's creepy. Jake's house never felt this way before. Look at Mister Numan; he's not a very nice man most of the time."

Angela said, "I've mostly been in places where I knew somebody. We must be going through your circle of friends, through scenes in your world."

"But the funnels are *random*, helloooo?"

"Yes... No," Angela blurted, "I... I don't know."

Zane looked away, scratching his chin. It felt itchy and he wondered if he could feel pain again, knowing that he could certainly feel heat and cold, and could hear. Even those voices he at least could hear. "Okay, I got it," he said and swung back. "We're in my circle now, connections to my life. Maybe that's why I hear the strange voice and you don't."

"Shush about the voice," Angela snarled.

"Okay," Zane breathed. He wondered what caused that reaction. Angela seemed stressed. Perhaps she really heard the voice and wouldn't admit it.

"Angela, do you think—"

"No I don't. Let's just watch and see what happens. Things only happen for those who wait."

Zane had no idea what that meant but all he could do was to hang around in this creepy house for something he knew deep down would probably be very unpleasant.

5: The Late Riser

Pete Numan groaned and rolled back onto his yellowed, slip-less pillow. He rubbed his eyes, flicking large crusts of sleep onto the sheets.

"Another day," he grumbled. He reached across the mattress and probed for his wife who wasn't there, then sat up and punched the mattress, a curious look on his face as he moaned, "Damn thing's so uncomfortable all of a sudden."

"Kathy!" he yelled down the hallway.

No reply.

"KATHY!" He struggled to stand. "Where's that woman?" He padded clumsily into the bathroom and flicked the light switch. The light was an intense glare and he caught a ghostly face in the shaving mirror. He stopped and gazed into his reflection.

"God, is that me?" He pulled at his sagging pallid cheeks, his face reflecting a moon glow, stark white and almost shiny like the bath tiles.

"I look lousy." He scratched his head, strands of carroty hair collecting in his fingers. He gave out a deep groan, thinking the hairline of his male pattern baldness had retreated a whole inch further in one night.

He stumbled into the walk-in robe and stooped over a pile of crumpled clothes.

"Kathy! Where's me ironed monkey suit?"

He picked up a crinkled shirt and trousers, holding them at arm's length before rejecting them, dumping them on the floor. "Darn forgot again," he cursed under breath. "Darn woman..."

"Jake!"

Again more silence.

"JAKE," he yelled at the top of his voice. "Must be at school already," he grumbled. "Look at the time!"

Zane felt relief and almost pleased not to see Jake here. Mister Numan was not always a pleasant man to meet whenever Zane visited and Jake always got an earful for seemingly trivial problems. The guy was stressed.

Zane glanced up and spotted Mister Numan looking straight at him.

Pushing a leaping heart aside, Zane told himself the man was looking past him and that made him feel a little more at ease.

"See?" Angela said with smugness in her eyes.

Mister Numan thrust his legs into his trousers. "Damn!" he cursed. "Why're these so uncomfortable? Felt okay yesterday.... Darn monkey suit's shrunk. KATHY!" he yelled, "What have you—" He stopped, mumbling something under his breath as he quickly scanned the chaotic bedroom.

"Whatsa use?"

Half-squeezed into his trousers, he hopped madly around the room in a struggle to pull them up to his waist.

A cockroach scampered gawkily over the shredded carpet pile. Numan stopped and scowled at it, then picked up a shoe and slammed it with the heel. The creature flexed in apparent pain, slowly fingering the air with one leg.

Numan crammed into his shoes which apparently also felt tight and noticed the cockroach struggling to make its escape. He stomped hard and stepped back to look with satisfaction, his grin dropping as the creature bumbled its way over the upturned coils of the frayed carpet. Numan stomped again and again but the roach refused to die.

"Darn things are built like tanks these days," he said and he cursed. "How many lives you got, eh?" He stomped again and counted, "... four, five, six," he breathed heavily, "seven... eight... nine... Blast you."

The roach stopped momentarily before swinging one bent antenna into the air.

"Are you giving me an 'up yours' gesture? Go to hell," he cursed, flicking the mangled creature with the tip of his shoe. Giving up, he probed the room for the rest of his clothes.

"Git offa there!" He flicked another roach off his coiled tie before looping it over his head.

"Ghastly man," Zane heard Angela say under her breath.

With loose tie and mismatched socks, Numan dashed down the corridor for the front door, only to stumble over a returning memory: "Bag, bag, bag, where, ah—" he spotted the black messenger bag and lunged for the vinyl handle. The bag seemed to pull back from his hand with added weight. He opened the bag slowly, wondering what could make it so heavy. Two pens, a folder, tablet device and his laptop sat where he had left them the night before. His zipped it tight and tried to pick it up again, only to have it leave his hand for the floor. He flung it open again and rubbed his chin. "What's making this thing so heavy? Sheesh, I need to work out some more."

Mister Numan heaved the bag up to his chest with both arms and awkwardly made for the car. "Damn darn it all, I bet Jake's back pack's lighter than this."

His cursing echoed down a silent suburban street, the air thick with smog.

He fumbled with the car key. Every time it went into the lock something would push it out again. "Now what..." he struggled further, finally jamming the key in with the back of another key. But now it would not turn.

Sweat streamed off his face on an unusually warm day. He threw off his jacket, annoyed at how it clung to him with a shrunken clammy embrace.

"Finally," he gasped as the key turned. He flung open the door and landed on a hot leather seat. "Damn darn and all hell," he cursed, jumping up and down. He grabbed his jacket and whisked it under his backside.

"Now," he breathed. He paused, holding the key over the ignition lock. He slowly inserted the key and it didn't bounce out as he thought it might. He carefully rotated it and the car started instantly. "Phew! Something's working," he gasped. He threw the gear stick into reverse and the car lunged forward.

"What the—" He slammed the brakes. At least they work, he thought fleetingly.

"Kathy, you done something to this car?" he wailed. "That's why you're not around, you..." He bashed both hands on the steering wheel and suddenly

61

opened his eyes with an idea. "That's it..." He threw the gear stick into Drive and the car instantly reversed out of the driveway, skidding, lurching onto the road. He flung the stick into Reverse and the car lunged forwards. "Right," he huffed. "Off to work."

Zane and Angela quickly slipped through the back doors of the car and rested on the back seat as Mister Numan sped down the road.

"Wonder how inertia works," Zane asked.

"Yes," Angela said, "I've wondered about this before. We can sit down and feel the seat under us … well, I can anyway—"

"Me too," he said quickly.

"And," she continued, "be moved by a solid object which we can pass through if we had to. It still amazes me."

"Who needs seat belts?" Zane laughed.

"If he brakes suddenly, we might fly into the car in front," she said, half amused.

"C'mon, c'mon," Mister Numan muttered. He wrenched the steering wheel to the left to get past a slow truck as they entered the freeway.

"At least we don't have to worry about being killed in a car accident," Zane said with a cynical chuckle.

"Yeah, but it's still scary," Angela said.

Zane suddenly lunged forward. "Stop the car!"

"What?" Angela shrieked. "You forget you're a dead duck again?"

"My home, my street – we're coming up to it!" Zane blurted. He poked his head through the window, catching sight of his house in the distance.

"Forget it," Angela said. "We're moving away from here and fast."

"But I can fly there, now!"

"No!" she said defiantly.

Zane wondered if she knew something he didn't. He looked back at the house as the car rounded a bend. No gardener, no postman and no Jack Russell terrier to yap at either of them. Gee I miss Mitch, he thought. I miss all of them. Jennifer must be at school. She must be there.

The house and street appeared silent, empty and almost lifeless in a sense. The autumn carpet from the tree-lined street stretched up to the front door. Mom would sweep the driveway, surely, he thought. The garage door, normally open was shut and the house gave Zane the impression no one had been there for years. He slumped back into the seat. There was no stopping, he knew that. "I'll have to go there sooner or later," he said glumly. "Something's wrong."

"We got bigger problems," Angela said flatly as she scanned the sky. "Notice something?"

"What?"

Angela slowly looked back at Zane, her face whiter than the ghostly white she had presented up until now.

The soft spirited haze had left her face and for the first time Zane could pick out the true color of her eyes, a deep color but not the almost blackish glaze he originally saw. They were deep green in shrouds of brown. He felt a shiver as he looked into those eyes. He quickly turned his gaze outside. He knew there was more to this new friend, and something about her disturbed him … but that was for solving later, he thought.

"Well, don't you see it?" she asked edgily.

"Don't see anything," he said, as if not listening.

She rolled her eyes at him. "That's the problem."

"Oh," he said casually, leaning back into the seat to glance up through the rear window. "No funnels, not a one." And then, with sudden realization, he sat upright. "No funnels!" His face now creased with concern. "But that means..."

"I've never been to a place without funnels," she said slowly.

"But we came here in one, so how do we get out? That one at Numan's wall stems from a different place –it'd be gone now."

"Zane, it never went through the wall, just met with it, and we were thrown through the wall."

"What's that mean?"

"Zane, this is really creeping me. We're supposed to be in your life's environment, your world. But there are no funnels here."

"Well, we saw them at my grave, but this place looks so weird now," he said, "so where have the funnels gone?"

"Shit damn!" cursed Mister Numan as he swung the car around an old Dodge moving at less than five miles per hour. "Darn obstacle race today!"

Angela scanned the sky and then looked at Zane, eyes wide with surprise. "No funnels."

Zane looked up and wondered how high he would have to go to find one. "We'll see one," he said as calmly as possible. "Soon, I reckon, probably in the city—" he stopped short, gaping at the traffic.

Angela saw it too. "The cars... so many different cars, like a parade..."

Then Mister Numan caught on. His jaw dropped as he approached the main freeway junction. Thousands of cars filled the eight lane freeway, late models rubbing fenders with old Chevrolets and vintage cars.

"A motor show?" he muttered. "Here?"

Angela spotted men on horseback, worming their way through the endless procession of steel and glass.

"Cowboys!" Zane exclaimed. "They're like cowboys!"

"Damn vintage carnival on today," Mister Numan cursed. "Why on a workday?" He rolled down his window to yell outside. "Doesn't anyone work anymore?"

Zane flung his head through the roof of the car. "They look so old but they look so new," he gasped.

"Where'd they all come from?"

"Who knows, Ange. Hey," he said, pointing, "That's like my dad's old Corvette but it looks brand new... must be worth a fortune."

"This is too weird," she said. "Something's wrong with this day, this place. Dumpster Man would know what's going on."

"Sure," Zane scoffed. "What's a trash man know about life and death?"

"Why did I choose to put up with you?" Angela growled. "You can be so annoying."

"Put up?" Zane frowned. "With me? Thanks. Hey, I didn't ask to die or go on a wild road trip with Jake's dad, or be teased by you." He fell back on the car seat and looked away glumly.

Angela stared blankly through her window and both sat silent as Mister Numan cursed and spat out of the window.

Zane knew Mister Numan was trouble. He knew Jake's mom had trouble staying with him and he knew Jake had trouble with both of them. Maybe I'll sit and listen, he thought. Maybe this'll go somewhere after all. Besides, I always wondered what Mister Numan did for a job. Jake never really talked about him, except to say he was a workaholic, a corporate climber, whatever that was.

Mister Numan weaved his car smoothly forward in reverse gear, dodging the traffic with ease. Other drivers appeared to be breaking the speed limit.

A whirring sound filled the car momentarily before tapering away. He glanced over his shoulder. A police car sped past, weaving through the traffic. It didn't appear to be chasing anyone. It just seemed to be speeding for the hell of it.

"Damn crazy roads," Numan huffed. He heaved a sigh of relief at the familiar sight of office towers and then he blinked hard and rubbed his eyes. The buildings appeared to be twice their size. His own office tower appeared to jut into infinity through reddened clouds. He stretched his neck back to look upwards as they approached the building. Arriving at the main entrance, he flung his head outside and gazed up to this strange glass obelisk that was his office. His lower back began to ache, the bones in his fingers clicking as he clutched the wheel. "What in Holy Mother of Mary's name is goin' on here?"

Zane and Angela slipped outside and stood awestruck at the immense size of the building.

"I haven't been to the city for a while," Zane said, "But it can't have changed that much."

"Look around you," Angela said slowly.

Zane stood gaping.

"Look, even Numan's confused," she said.

"I'm sick," Numan muttered. "That's it, sick. Maybe I'll blink and find myself back in bed. Blame all that booze last night with the advertising guys." He squirmed in his seat and wondered how it had become so uncomfortable.

The wheel suddenly jerked free of his grip and the car jolted onto the sidewalk.

"JESUS!"

Numan threw the gear into Park and yanked the handbrake and then noticed what Angela and Zane had already noticed. Cars were parked all over the place, haphazardly down the road and on the sidewalk.

"Hah," Numan sniffed. "When in Rome." He stumbled out of the car, leaving it skewed partly across the sidewalk and gutter.

He stood gawking up at his building which had appeared to grow many more floors overnight. Low smog clouds shrouded the upper floors. He strained his eyes to see as a window opened just below the cloud line.

Mister Numan flung open the passenger door and fished in his pocket for his cell phone. He leaned against the open door and held the phone to his eye as steadily as possible, pressing the zoom button and aiming the cross-hatch to the window high above. He could barely make out the shape of a person jutting out from the window.

Numan gulped. "Stuart Anglis?" He stood upright and stumbled back as pedestrians muscled their way past him.

"Stuey, no!" he yelled. "No, Stuey, NO!"

Stuart Anglis, office buddy, now hung precariously from the window ledge. Half his body protruded to air, held by a single arm in a pinstriped sleeve.

Mister Numan felt a crack in his neck as he arched back and waved furiously. "Stuey... *Stuey!*"

His cry fell on deaf ears. Pedestrians streamed past him, ignoring the drama above. Some people clambered over the scatter of cars parked in their way. Shoulder bags, briefcases and handbags hammered others aside.

Numan uttered a high-pitch curdling scream.

Zane and Angela shrank back as the shrilling reverberated through them. Despite the scream, no one on the street seemed to notice. Zane looked up to the wide-eyed and wind-blown man falling towards them.

Stuart Anglis fell to his death.

6: Dead on Schedule

"Whoa!" Zane flew in front of Angela, trying to distract, if not block to some degree, her view of a dead body on the sidewalk.

"Zane! What are you doing?" She shot around him, returning her eyes to the doughy mound that was Stuart Anglis.

"I..."

"Don't look," Zane insisted. "Haven't we seen enough death?"

"I'm okay," she said, but I don't think Mister Numan is."

Dumbfounded, Mister Numan gaped at the body and then jerked himself away, stumbling back towards the main foyer. He didn't notice the change in architecture, his mind scissoring out his foreground to replace it with an image of a howling Stuart Anglis falling through the air. He staggered slowly, bumping past pedestrians who ignored the crumpled body. One elderly pedestrian stepped on the bloodied jacket and kept walking, seemingly oblivious to the obstruction.

"He wanted to leave his mark at this company," Mister Numan chuckled to himself. It was an awkward, sickly chuckle and he choked on his words. "He wanted to make an impact. " He chuckled louder.

"He's losing it," Angela said.

"Think I know how he feels," Zane replied. "Why don't people here care? Where's the ambulance, the cops? Why doesn't that guard *do* something?"

Angela tilted her head sideways with dazed eyes. "Don't know," she said slowly. "Things have changed and I can't believe your life's world is like this. Look at Mister Numan. He at least appears affected."

Mister Numan swallowed hard and blinked, approaching the metal doors. "What's this?" he asked of a guard.

"Tightened security, terrorism and all that," the guard said with a cold stare from an acne-scarred face. He frowned. "You should be used to this by now. Been drinking again?" He pointed with his gun. "Step on the platform, sir."

Numan scratched his head as the guard motioned to a plate of glass embedded in the concrete vestibule.

"I don't remember this being here yesterday." He stepped onto the tinted glass and wondered what it was. A beam of light panned across the glass from underneath, scanning his shoes, which turned blue momentarily. "Hah, wow," he muttered.

"TPS clear," the guard said and motion him forward.

"TPS?"

"Toe Print Scan," the guard said, shaking his head. The shiny metal foyer doors rumbled open and Mister Numan hesitantly stepped through.

Angela and Zane followed. "Glad we don't have to worry about security," Zane said.

Mister Numan entered the foyer and looked back at the doors. He scratched his head. "Huh?"

Zane looked at the doors and could see through them into the street, even though the doors appeared as solid metal from the outside. "This building's strange, like futuristic."

Angela's eyes widened. "We're in the future – your world's future!" she exclaimed.

"Don't be daft," Zane scoffed. "How can we time travel?"

Angela shrugged, brushing aside her rusty red fringe. "Don't know; never done it before but there's always a first. I think the Dumpster Man said it could happen from the funnels and, yeah, I remember him talking about time travel of a sort but when I asked for more info he clammed up. So, Zane, what about all those old cars out there, huh? What about them?"

"Yeah, but they're old cars, that's *back* in time." He shook his head, getting more confused and agitated by his surroundings. "So if we time traveled, are we back in time or forward?"

Angela shrugged again. "Old things come back in fashion. Anyway, let's see how Mister Numan copes. He seems just as confused as we are and he's from this place."

"Sure, and he doesn't look any older than I remember him, so the future and all this with him here is baffling me silly," Zane said nervously. "It's all messed up."

"Money," Mister Numan muttered. "Make money, that'll get my mind off him." He bumped into a lady, a bundle of tattered-looking files spilling from her arms. One folder slipped through the cavity between the elevator and the foyer.

"That's clever, Pete" she said. "But thanks. I don't have to worry about giving something up-to-date to Mister Smars. I'll just say it's lost. Everything's lost; I'm lost," she rambled.

"Sorry, Sally," he replied.

"Well, are you going to block my way to the elevator now?"

"Sorry."

"Yeah, people still say 'Sorry, Sally'," she huffed, brushing her blonde hair aside. "Sorry I stepped on your toe, Sally. Sorry I stuck that pencil in your ear, Sally. Oh yeah, everyone's sorry —not." She entered the elevator with Mister Numan and elbowed a button. "Twenty four as usual?"

Mister Numan stood motionless, his face numb from the death of Anglis.

"Stop floating off somewhere, Pete," Sally said. "Remember those new company policies. Be alert."

Mister Numan turned slowly and offered a weak frown at the lanky woman. "What policies?"

She dropped her files and mockingly drilled a finger into the side of her head. "You okay upstairs?"

"Sure," he coughed. "Sure I am."

"Good," she said quickly. "Those new company policies are important, as are the new management policies."

"You should care," Numan mumbled. "Not giving a toss about losing an important file."

"What?"

His eyes opened quickly. "What management policies?"

"Don't play tricks with me, Pete. I'm not in the mood. You know all about the takeover. You're scheduled to meet him today."

"Him?"

"Your new boss, stupid!"

Mister Numan coughed. "Right, err … of course, forgot about that, late night and all."

"And I suppose you've forgotten about us?" she said and scowled. "Or have you had another guilt trip over your wife?"

Zane glanced at Angela.

"Sorry, I don't love you anymore, Sally," she continued. "Sorry I spat out your meal, Sally. Sorry—"

"Okay, okay!" Mister Numan said, hushing the air with his hands. "Those drinks last night can be damning. You know how it is." He scratched his head. "Like, err..." he quickly looked around, "like I don't remember renovations to this elevator. A glass elevator's real hip these days. It's really interesting seeing all those floors around us as we go up. Bit unsafe that indoor shaft where there's no wall, cutting... through the floors from..." his voice slowed with rising confusion, "...ground to top level..."

"Where you been?" She glared at him, tossing her blonde hair away from cold brown eyes. "On another planet?"

"No," Numan said, shrugging. "Not that I can remember."

"My, you have lost it, haven't you?" She smiled slightly. "Don't worry, my dear." She touched his arm. "Since the air conditioning was removed, that shaft facilitates a great cost-cutting, greenhouse-savvy breeze."

Mister Numan shook his head in disbelief. "A five yard or so gap I can see from floor edge to glass wall that stretches across one side of the building, without a protective railing? That's nuts. Don't remember that yesterday," he scratched his head again and rolled his eyes with uncertainty, "but I *feel* like I do."

Sally picked up her files and gave a smug look. "It's called a 'Dead Line', a great way to encourage competition."

Mister Numan fell back against the elevator wall. "This doesn't make sense at all," he mumbled. "Why doesn't each floor meet all walls? Why the gap all the way to the bottom? I don't remember this elevator shaft, or the security entrance for that matter, but why does this whole thing feel normal to me?"

Sally ignored him.

The elevator jolted to a stop and the glass doors quietly slid apart. Mister Numan scanned the plush office. Some desks appeared rearranged. "Where's Warrick?"

"Hasn't arrived here yet."

"And Steve?"

"Oh, you won't see him here," she said coolly.

Mister Numan opened his mouth to ask why and then swallowed hard. Somehow he knew he wouldn't be seeing Steve at all, not ever, but he just couldn't figure out how he knew or why.

"See ya later," Sally said firmly as she took a right-hand turn down a dim corridor.

Mister Numan strode past his secretary, expecting her to blow him a kiss good morning. Instead, she remained head-down, her blank face glowing in front of the computer screen.

Something's wrong, he pondered. Maybe I'll get the sack for something. He flung open his office door and stopped, staring at the floor. The green carpet stretched past his desk. The wall that was behind his desk had now been set back and a shaft gaped between. He approached his desk slowly and leaned over slightly to peer down the shaft. He counted twenty three slabs of concrete floors below him. The wall that should have been behind his desk was now offset by the shaft by some five yards or so. Warm air fanned his face as he gazed at the movements of office workers along the edges of each floor. Feeling dizzy, he leaned back onto his desk and rummaged through the top drawer. Producing a pen, he held it over the ledge and let go. The pen rotated slowly in the air until finally pinging on the ground floor.

"Pete."

Mister Numan tipped clumsily as he swung to face his caller.

The man facing Mister Numan grinned mischievously. His sports jacket and shirt were stained. It was a dark stain. Blood. His crumpled face sagged against the bone, the skin flapping like wet leather, his gray eyes bloodshot and bulging from their sockets.

Mister Numan shuddered, his lips quivering as he tried to spit out the words. "Stuey... Stuart Anglis!"

7: Takeover

"I've been demoted," Anglis whined, his sagging face now turning sour with a sickly yellow.

"STAY BACK!" Numan screamed, "You're dead, you're bloody DEAD!"

"But, Pete..." Stuart drooled slowly. He stood in the doorway, his face streaming with tears.

A shadow drew from behind him and a dark blue pinstripe sleeve appeared; a large sun-tanned hand rested on Stuart's shoulder. "Now-now, mah dear Mister Anglis, we can't have this," a voice spoke from behind with a slight Southern drawl that resonated throughout the office.

Zane and Angela dashed behind the filing cabinet, both feeling a certain dread – the kind of dread they had never felt before. They looked at each other, aware of their shared fears. They didn't quite know why they should feel afraid of a living person.

"Go down to your new cubicle on Level 22, Mister Anglis," said the voice, reassuringly. "The sec'a'tary will be a-waitin' for you there. She may even be free this evening."

Anglis stepped aside to reveal the stranger standing behind. Anglis chuckled slowly, his chuckling broken by gasps for air. He forced a smile at Mister Numan, his dangling jowls swinging with the rising, sickly smile. "Always on your back, they say. Nice working with you Pete. See ya 'round."

Mister Anglis turned for the door as the pinstriped stranger slapped him on the shoulder and grinned mischievously, offering a sly chuckle.

Angela squinted to see through the filing cabinet as her ghost partly melded with it.

"How can a dead guy come to life?" Zane asked.

"Don't know," she whispered.

"I'd like to know," Zane said quietly, "I died too early; well, that's how I feel. It'd be nice to be alive again."

"You sure?" Angela asked, thinking she'd rather be dead than alive in this place.

"Hey, think Mister Numan will get the sack? Wonder what Jake'll do if his dad is unemployed and home all the time. He'd go nuts."

"Shush!" She looked Zane squarely in the eyes as if knowing something he didn't, her face glazed with terror. "I don't think Jake's within a million miles of this place."

"What the—"

"I just feel it."

"How? How could you know, Ange?"

"Just a feeling I got – a strong feeling."

The pinstriped stranger folded his arms as he gazed around the office. His neat deep blue pinstriped suit and wide collar gave him the air of some eccentric robber baron or perhaps a gangster, Zane thought.

"Hmm, nice awffice you have, sir," the stranger spoke, his voice lowering. "Too nice." His grin dropped instantly and he glared at Mister Numan. "You're late, Numan," he huffed, "but it's your first day. So wee'll be a tad harder on you."

Mister Numan fell back onto his swivel chair, forgetting the shaft behind him.

The well-dressed stranger approached him, hand outstretched, the elastic grin returning. "I'm Harry Abaddon," he said firmly, "but you sir can call me Old Harry."

The clasp was warm. Mister Numan had never shaken a warmer hand and, as he withdrew, the skin on his palm grated like sandpaper. Old Harry stood shorter than Mister Numan. His shirt was a blazing white and Numan had to look away. Old Harry's gray goatee wiggled with every word and Numan somehow knew that canyon-aged face under a crown of short curly gray hairs could tell a thousand tales.

Numan swallowed hard and tried to recover his wits, as he straightened his tie. "What do you mean... it's my first day? I've been working here for years!" he protested.

Old Harry grunted and paced the length of Numan's office, then took a peek at the floors below him. On Level 22, he spied Mister Anglis heaving a slab of concrete and a bag of cement on a trolley. "I say, what you doing down there?" he yelled.

"Department head told me to fix the sidewalk," Anglis bawled.

Old Harry swung back to face the indignant look on Mister Numan's face. "Weell, sir, there have been many changes, as you can see," – he opened his hands – "though you are alreedy becoming a'customized to them." He then repeatedly stabbed the air with his finger in Numan's direction as he spoke. "The name of the game is still the same, son, though the objective," his bloodshot eyes widened, "is somewhat different."

"W-What..." Numan stammered, "what you mean?"

Angela could tell Numan was now more nervous than ever. Everything that had happened to him this day had been incredible but he had held his own ground, dismissing everything around him like some bizarre clown show.

Zane could see it too. He glanced at Angela. "Why do I feel freaked by this?"

"Because this place is a freak show," she replied.

Old Harry huffed. "What dooh I mean, Numan? Weell," he paced again. "You know you must get to the top. That's always a pri-ority, though you may ne'er make it." He probed his pocket and produced a fob watch on a fat chain, a chunky timepiece with a dozen or more hands circling the dial. A haze of colored light slithered off the watch face and onto his hand, throwing a curly zebra pattern of violet, yellow and blue across his jacket.

Angela squinted to see.

Zane spotted her looking at the watch intensely. "Pretty neat watch, huh?"

"Who cares about a dumb watch," she said flatly. "That Harry guy is scaring me."

"Say," Zane said, looking at her quizzically for a moment, "what's he gonna do to Numan?"

Angela kept staring in Old Harry's direction.

Zane prodded her. "Ange?"

"Huh?"

"What do you think he'll do to Numan?"

"Got a bad feeling about this," she said urgently.

Old Harry whisked a handkerchief from his top pocket and wiped the face of the watch. A row of tiny multicolored lights flashed around the circumference of the watch face, their reflections glinting on the metal rim and polished chrome buttons that jutted from the sides, the entire array of lights offering a mini rainbow effect across the walls of the office. Harry pushed on a button and a red-colored hand swung into motion, clicking as it arced to meet a matching red light on the dial which began to flash faster. Old Harry nodded slowly before pocketing the watch. He glanced in the direction of the filing cabinet for a moment, then back at Numan.

Zane gulped and slipped a bit further behind the cabinet, burning his eyes through the metal to see.

Numan was too busy dreading his possible demise to take interest in the watch. "Why won't I make it?" he asked, almost defiantly.

Old Harry patted the pocket that contained the fob watch and continued pacing the office. "Hmmm, they say only one person made it to the top from here." He suddenly swung to look Mister Numan directly in the eyes. "But not you sir, oooh no, you old dawg. Oh, but by all means try." He laughed, his face contorting those canyon lines as loose skin flaked off like paste from a clown's makeup.

"You've been given a real sweet pay rise."

A slight smile nudged across Mister Numan's face.

"Though," Old Harry sighed, "Money these days just 'int what it used to be."

Numan's smile instantly dropped.

"You'll hate everything you buy," Old Harry breathed. "But you can have anything you want," he said lightly and he waved his arms, "women, wine, food aplenty. But you won't enjoy it."

Numan swallowed hard, sweat beading down his forehead.

Old Harry peered down the shaft again. "You see, Numan, what you eat will be tasteless. If it has a taste, you'll be paying through the nose for the taste of rottin' meat and moldy bread."

Mister Numan sat bewildered. "I... I don't get it."

"Really now?" Old Harry's pointed eyebrows rose with faint surprise. "It's really quite simple, mah dear Mister Numan." He narrowed his eyes. "*Think about it.*"

Numan glanced around the office, then at the shaft. "Ye-yesterday was so fresh in my mind, so invigorating. I had fun yesterday. Today, well, everything feels normal and... and looks normal in a way, but it's sort of different in a normal way, heh—" he chuckled wryly, "And I hate every minute of it."

87

"Good!" Old Harry breathed, clapping his hands. "*Good!* That's what I want to see." His eyes lit a fiery red as he pulled out a cigar from his top pocket.

Mister Numan watched the odd man place one end of the cigar in the palm of his hand rotating it slowly. It lit instantly.

Total fear now rippled through Numan's body, the swivel chair underneath him edging closer to the ledge.

Old Harry lunged toward him, thrashing both hands onto the old oak desktop. His face now darkened to a burgundy color, searing the impression of ages into Numan's eyes.

Numan's chair rattled as he sat quivering at the ferocity before him.

Zane and Angela sunk back further into the filing cabinet, peering through a partially open draw for better vision.

Old Harry glared at Numan with blood-shot anger. "Don't you know where you are, boy?" He puffed importantly, blowing smoke into Numan's ashen face as the chair underneath creaked back another inch.

Numan gulped. "I... err—"

"You're *DEAD!*" Old Harry suddenly roared.

Numan shuddered, his chair jerking underneath. "D-d-dead?"

"Ayuh, Mister Numan, dead!" Harry cried. "Dead like that dawg you hit in the street last week. Dead like that Carter kid your son Jake used to play with. Dead like the man who blackmailed you with photos of you an' Sally. Dead, dead, DEAD! But don' worry, you'll see him again. He's on Level 11. Look down..."

Zane gaped at Angela. "He's dead, like us... and Old Harry knows about me!"

"He can't see us," Angela said quickly, "I think—"

"But maybe he knows we're here!" Zane shrieked.

"Shush, Zane, I don't know for sure but maybe he can hear us."

"I said *look*, Numan," Old Harry roared, "Look hard..."

An invisible force seemed to grab hold of Numan's head, forcing him to contort his neck awkwardly to peer down the shaft. The carpeted concrete slab of Level 11 rumbled, slowly sliding across to block the shaft at that level. The various office workers on that level seemed oblivious to the fact that their floor had moved.

Old Harry slid across the desk and grabbed the arms of Mister Numan's swivel chair.

"Wh-wh-wh-what are you doing?" Numan stammered.

"Must give you a head start," Harry breathed.

"Wait! Where's my wife?"

Old Harry swung off the desk. As he did so, a spiked red tail dropped from his backside, thudding on the carpet. He clutched Numan's collar and breathed smoke in his eyes – and he hadn't taken a puff from his cigar that time. He gripped Numan's chin which wobbled like jelly, jerking his head upwards to the floors above. Hundreds of levels stretched to a pinprick in the sky. "She's up there," he breathed.

"How can that be? She's alive, and-and h-happy at home."

"Happy? HAPPY?" Old Harry growled. "My, you have a nerve." He cleared his throat. "Time is irrelevant here. Your wife is awaaays up there. Now you have to work hard to reach the boss upstairs and you know you won't. But try hard, my dear Mister Numan." He flicked a glance towards the filing cabinet and then swung back at Numan. "You were real late this mornin'," he snapped. "And now you will be demoted to Level Eleven."

"No," Numan wailed, "Wait!"

Old Harry levered his pointed and overly-polished black crocodile skin shoe under the wheel arches of Numan's chair, flicking it up with ease. Both man and chair fell, Numan's scream cut short by the ruptured echo of metal and leather against skin, bone and the concrete under carpet that is Level Eleven.

Old Harry slicked back his hair with the back of his hand and leaned over to observe the sprawled remains of man and chair. He tapped ash from his cigar over the ledge before flicking the end into the air, then cupped his mouth in his hands and cried, "Weelcome to Hades my friend. Don' worry about death. You're already dead in this place an' I can whop your ass as often as it pleases me. But don' fret, Mister Numan, you can ne'er really die, you know, no matter how many times you fall."

Angela grabbed Zane's arm. "This place is full of dead people. This place must be Hell!" She pulled him towards the wall behind the filing cabinet where they slipped into the cavity. Both squinted to see back through the wall at Old Harry.

"It's a weird hell," Zane whispered. "Not what I expected."

"Must be Mister Numan's hell," Angela said. "That's it… gotta be. It's all about him, it's all around him. That's why no one can see us."

"Whatever it is, I want out. Anyway, so why couldn't all those dead people we passed outside see *us*?"

91

"Because it's gotta be *Mister Numan's* hell," Angela insisted. "And maybe everyone else here has the same attitude as Mister Numan, a rat-race attitude. I don't know. And why are you still whispering? We're further away from Old Harry."

Zane aimed a shaky finger. "That's why."

Old Harry stared with narrow eyes at the wall in their direction.

"I knew he could see us," Zane whispered quickly.

"He couldn't before," Angela replied.

"Well he can now!" Zane screeched.

Old Harry carefully approached the wall, stretching out his hand which held the pocket watch. "Numan's wretched density," he cursed. "C'mon, show yourselves..."

The watch glowed more fiercely and the wall began to sear, bubble and tear away like burning paper.

"Dive," Angela yelled, "Dive down through the floors!"

"I know you're there," growled the voice of Abaddon behind them.

Zane and Angela drilled themselves down through concrete floor after concrete floor until a cushioning feeling suddenly smothered them, pressing softly, as if they had fallen onto a soft bed.

"Fools!" cried the fading voice behind them.

"Holy crap, Ange!"

"A funnel," Angela yelped. "We're in a funnel and away from that place!"

"That was too close," Zane said, as he acknowledged the marshmallow-like walls of the funnel, "This one's bright. Could be a much better place we're going to. How'd we find it, anyway?"

"I'm not sure how we escaped that Hell," she said. "I felt like something yanked us into the funnel, just at the last minute."

"Or pushed us?" Zane asked quizzically. "Amazed we found a funnel in the first place – couldn't see them anywhere in that place. Say, think that Harry or devil or whatever he is will come after us?"

"Doubt it," she said hesitantly. "He'd have to find the right funnel and as they move all the time…"

"Hopefully he won't. As you say, maybe there aren't many at all back there," Zane said, as he stretched his gaze behind him.

"I think we're safe," she said with a slight tremor in her voice.

"That devil guy, was he for real?"

"Real enough for Mister Numan," she replied. "And he sure scared the hell out of me."

"Something else weird about that stinkin' place," Zane said. "I just hope Jake isn't involved. I hope you're right and Jake's a million miles away. If Mister Numan is dead, he must've died soon after my death... but how?"

"We may never know," Angela said softly.

A distant blackness at the end of the funnel caught Zane's attention. It momentarily came into view and then disappeared again as the ribbed and cloudy funnel walls swayed their curves to block the view. They swept effortlessly around the curves despite the thrashing and Angela then spotted the blackness too.

"Funnel exit coming up," she said.

"*...You are so glum...*"

"That stinkin' voice is back," Zane cursed. "It's here in this funnel. Seems to happen when we're about to enter a place."

"You're freaking me again," Angela said, "As if that last place wasn't scary enough. Like nowhere I've been before, so real but unreal."

The ribbed walls of the funnel suddenly tore apart to open sky.

Zane looked down to a carpet of soft clouds. They reflected a soft moonlight glow but when he looked up he could see no moon, only blackness. "Wow, we're high," he remarked. "Scary, being high, like in a jumbo jet, but without the jet."

"You're trembling, Zane. Thought you liked flying," she said. "Or are you still shook up over that devil guy? We're a long way from that place, I'm sure."

"I know," he said slowly, "It's this place. I don't see any stars above us."

"Travel can be disorientating," Angela said. "And the Dumpster Man said ghosts have more trouble orientating with gravity. Let's head for the clouds until our eyes adjust to this light. We could be upside down for all we know and the ground is above us."

Zane shook his head. "Dumpster Man, yeah right."

Angela ignored him as they swooped towards the clouds.

The cloud light appeared to dim the closer they approached. They jutted through the momentary thickness, the clouds breaking apart.

Zane tried to get a bearing, expecting to see stars but there was nothing. Total blackness gaped back at them. Zane could not redirect his eyes from the abyss. There was nothing there, nothing at all.

8: Causality Casualty

Nothing but blackness gaped at them. Angela glanced behind and couldn't see the clouds they had just passed through. She guessed the light must have come from somewhere on the other side and wondered how fast they were traveling as friction was another confusing element, according to the Dumpster Man. But she wasn't going to mention that to Zane for now. He's new, she thought, new to all this, but I'm not much older at it and every new place is a new experience for both of us.

She began to feel numb and reached out to Zane's hand for some kind of touch, just to touch anything. Touching Zane was awkward in itself; the tingling sensation from before was intriguing but she could sense a whole world of unfamiliar thoughts and perceptions, boy thoughts that made her want to tread carefully for some reason. He's tense and uncertain, she mused, and immature, but in the blackness he was the only real thing around and perhaps he needed guidance like a younger brother might do, if she had a younger brother. But now she didn't feel so confident and felt awkward instead, hesitantly holding her arm out but retracting her fingers from his glowing edges.

She turned to gaze into the void and imagined what it would be like to visit the universe before the universe began. Would it be like this, even before the start of the big light that led to the Big Bang? What would they know, the scientists, anyway? She glanced at Zane who appeared not to notice her reach. "Right now this is our universe," she said. "Nothing else exists as far as we can see. Anything before doesn't *matter*."

"My mind wants to put things here," Zane said slowly as he gaped at the blackness, "like trees, houses, roads and so on. I can look over there and see a tree, because it's so dark my mind can just fill it with something, and maybe, if I don't concentrate, only horrible things may come from my subconscious, like monsters."

"Don't be silly," she said. "I kind of love this black nothing. I don't know where we're going and I can't even tell if we're moving or not. Why do you see monsters, Zany?"

"Don't do that!" He glared at her. "That supposed to be funny? We're in this nothing place and you can make jokes about my name? Maybe this is Nickname Hell. Some hell... may as well be Nothing Hell as I didn't have much going on in my life, especially since Dad took off. He used to say I was a big no-good stinkin' nothing. So nothing's my future."

"Only if you believe it," Angela said.

"Yeah, right, this is my hell," Zane said quietly. "This is where I get off – right here."

"What do you mean – get off here?"

"A fitting end for a pointless guy like me."

"You're so glum," Angela huffed.

"Glum? That's what the voice said, that stupid crusty voice coming from nowhere—"

"...*Glum...*" the voice uttered hollowly in the dark.

Zane quivered, his soft glow rippling around the edges. "There's three of us here!"

"You're completely mad, Zane. Why I bother traveling with you..."

Zane shook his head vigorously and wondered why Angela couldn't hear it. He knew the voice had followed them into the void but he couldn't fathom its presence, a voice with no body, let alone apparition. Now here with him! He couldn't understand how it could possibly follow them through the entrance to this blackness but he refused to believe he was going insane.

He stared into the pitch void and imagined being home with Mom, Jen and Mitch. He could clearly see the house in the distance, Mitch dancing for attention in the front yard and Jennifer tossing him the biggest ball he could get his teeth around. He wanted to go home. He wanted to be where he was before. He reached out for the image before him, imagining it to be at the other end of a funnel. Home, he thought, the only place I know. And then the distant image of his father returned, his face enraged as he burst through the front door, ripping off his tie and flinging his jacket to the sofa. It was a short flicker of memory that tingled down his ghostly spine. And then the flash and rumble of orange clouds returned, lighting the sky in his mind's eye.

"You're right, Zane," Angela said, "This place isn't empty after all."

The image before Zane instantly dissolved. He blinked hard and swung to look down, expecting the owner of that voice to materialize into some kind of human or ghostly form. But Angela was pointing to something else.

"There's ground down there," she said. "If only we had bigger eyes to see better in the dark."

"...*Glum*..." the voice uttered.

"Not empty up here either," Zane moaned.

Angela ignored him. "Look, I can see small fires!"

Zane picked out the tiny yellow dots in the blackness and wondered how Angela could see the ground at all. However, the further down they flew the more they could see in the night sky. Zane wondered if the influence of the funnel they left was still around them, only dispersed much wider in the sky so as to mostly block out the natural light.

They swept downwards towards the jagged outlines of dimly lit hillsides that appeared to be split by an earthquake. Angela suddenly stopped, her arm swinging out to hold Zane back. "God!"

They could see better now but now wished they hadn't. Gray soil stretched for miles into the distance, crisscrossed by a random mesh of barbed wire. Thousands of bodies lay scattered across the cindered landscape. Tanks stood still like tilted obelisks in the half-light, their metal casings ripped apart, curled raggedly at the edges like torn cardboard. Zane imagined their jagged silhouettes jutting out of the ground like giant gravestones.

Angela tugged at his arm. "Let's go."

He shrugged. "Why?"

"Let's go!"

"Where?" He looked down upon the feeble glow of his spirit. It was fainter now, almost defeated by shock and disappointment. He could feel the energy being drained by his emotions. Angela could feel it too. Their tiny glows spilled onto the mangled, bloody bodies of soldiers cast aside like toys. Their bodies were splayed against the shoulders of others in different uniform. Zane couldn't recognize any of the insignia.

Papers fluttered in a wind that had the stench of cleaning solvent. Angela caught a pair of bloodied eyes staring blankly into the night and she quickly turned away. Open-mouthed, another face appeared to gawk at Zane. It was sunken, as if the skin was blasted off by intense heat. Two holes where the eyes used to be contained partly-dissolved skin which also sagged below the chin, making it appear abnormally long. His arm was outstretched in a tattered sleeve, a gas mask resting two or three inches beyond reach.

"Too late," Zane said quietly.

"*Zane,*" Angela said urgently, "Hey!" She shook him hard, her hands throbbing as they sank into his frozen form. "Let's go!"

Zane looked up at her slowly. "Did this just happen? I feel like I'm in a kind of death zone frozen in time. It's a dead man's land. When did all this happen?"

"How should I know?"

"And where are all their ghosts?"

"Gone," she said with sour eyes.

Zane folded his arms and stared into the distance. "Gone elsewhere, like us? And where are we, anyway?"

"What does it matter?" she said softly. "C'mon."

They slowly arced up into the dark sky above.

Zane looked behind to the shadowy mounds. "Why do people believe in God, when all they get, over and over again, is that?"

"Dunno, Zane. Hey, maybe you 'n me are here to find out?"

"Oh, sure," Zane scoffed, "you think we're guided by something? You think there's a stinkin' God? Well, I haven't seen him. You think he would have wanted us to behave like this? People make their own mistakes and that's that. War is so dumb." He sighed heavily. "Patriotism's like a fishing net, trawling people together to be eaten by the privileged few who like to play toy soldiers."

Angela folded her arms. "Something your Dad said?" She looked behind her but now the darkness had returned. She could make out the thin arc of the horizon and wondered how far this war had gone.

"It makes me so angry…" Zane blurted, "I … I could shoot someone! Hah!"

"That's a bad joke, Zane."

"Dad always said sometimes humor helps and maybe a stupid war can be laughable. He always talked about atomic wars. Grew up in that time of fear I guess. Somehow rubbed off on me, so I gotta laugh, see?"

"War can never be laughable," Angela said, narrowing her eyes, "nor can a stupid wasteful death, although in your case it might be funny."

Zane fired a suspicious look at her and felt she knew a little more about his death than he did, as grasping at the images was difficult. Over and over he tried to piece the scenario of his demise but it floated just beyond reach. Mitch's face fleetingly filled his mind's eye, that slopping tongue, big brown eyes and kicking legs stealing all concentration from the hurtling death that brought him here. He looked away. The other dog suddenly came into prominence, a bulky and ripple-skinned creature with a dangling, saliva-flicking tongue constantly barking, not seeming to care about its stretched and throaty vocal chords, the sand-papery voice shrilling through Zane's ears…

Look at something else, Zane thought. Look at something here…

He swung about and glared at Angela. "What do you know that I don't know?" he demanded. "How could you know anything?"

"People at your funeral talked," she said. "They said you did a dumb thing."

"I don't care," he blurted. "I don't know why I don't care, I just..." He stopped and folded his arms, offering a suspicious look. "Just how long were you hanging around my funeral anyways?"

Angela turned away.

Zane also looked away, probing his mind for more images in the puzzle. He swung back at her. "So remind me then," he said shakily. "Tell me the gross details."

"I don't know much more myself," Angela said. "All I could hear them say was your death was a terrible, stupid waste. Someone said you should've seen it coming, but they didn't say what."

"A car hit me?"

"No, they didn't say." Angela quickly turned away and Zane heard her grumble, "I hate cars."

Zane felt another tear push for attention but this time it was a tear for his family. "So I must have done a dumb thing."

"Look ahead dummy duck," Angela said, "Lights on the hillside!"

Zane thought about how precarious life was, how one second everything seemed hunky dory then the next it was gone in a flash, either from a stupid mistake or a fate that was to come, anyway – and perhaps fate and stupidity are often the same. "Too late to think about it now, I guess."

He blinked and noticed that Angela had left his side. "Hey, wait up!"

Her glow had taken for the lights and Zane caught up with her as they lost altitude, now zigzagging diagonally through rows and rows of pine trees. He trailed just behind her, glancing back at the black hills on the horizon that masked the fields of dead soldiers. Zane felt sure he could see them more clearly if the moon was up but thanked himself there was nothing shining in the sky that night. Darkness can hide a lot, he thought.

"Zane! Get out of Self Pity City and come here," Angela demanded.

"Coming," he said, rolling his eyes.

She hovered over a small stone church just ahead of the trees and they noticed the colors of stained glass glowing from a soft inner light that seemed welcoming. Zane felt the warmth strangely envelop him. It's just a building, he thought, but right now it felt like the most comforting place to be.

Angela brushed Zane's side to see through the stained glass. The tingling of her passing touch caused them to look at each other momentarily.

They hovered outside the window and peered inside. "Well someone's alive in this land," she said. "Perhaps we could find out what's going on here."

Zane strained his eyes to see through the colored glass as images began to cloud his vision, images of his mother running down the driveway screaming at Dad in his beat-up station wagon. He ignored her as she grappled with the driver's door, watching him yank it away from her and then hammering the accelerator and skidding out of the driveway, narrowly missing the mailbox.

And then the voice returned, causing Zane to shudder and blink hard, recapturing his surroundings only to look away from Angela who seemed not to notice him anyway, as more eerie words resonated through his head. As usual, Angela didn't seem to hear the voice. The words were meant for him...

"Oh lost soul, you are so glum,
To learn so much yet rise to none,
You really have lost all directions,
Falling short of best intentions..."

Zane clutched his head with both hands and swayed in the air. A chill seemed to clutch his stomach and spread out through his limbs as if someone was jerking him awake from a deep sleep. He crammed his eyes shut then flicked them hard open. Ignore and concentrate on something else, he thought. Ignore and watch what Angela does. Maybe the voice will leave me alone, if I am not waiting to hear it. He looked inside the church. Bleary-eyed, he watched an old priest or perhaps minister striding across a well-polished floor, waving his arms in the air to nobody.

"We are victims of our own causality," the minster grumbled to himself. He slowed his pace and looked upwards.

Angela slipped through the stained glass to watch from near the vestry, and then jutted her arm out through the window to reach Zane. "Hey, you're suddenly a bit harder to touch now, like you're fading away," she said with concern.

"Okay," Zane said, breathing hard, "I'm okay. Felt like I was being drawn away – in fact, more like *drained* away." He released a yawn. "I'm fine now." He forced a grin and Angela tilted her head in curiosity then smiled cautiously in return as his freckly face resolved to fullness.

Zane probed his mind for the last strands of that voice but the words were now gone. The coldness that clasped his stomach had released and he let out a sigh along with it as he tried to gather his surroundings. He floated down to the church entrance as the minster mumbled to himself.

Angela followed and they both spotted the notice board covered in the usual church notices and a large flyer pinned over some of the others. A picture of the minister was printed on the flyer, a much younger-looking man by the name of Pastor Cavanaugh.

"Kirchplatzl Baptist church," Angela read slowly, "wherever that is. Worship services on the twenty seventh cancelled."

"Because of the war?"

Angela caught Zane's quizzical frozen eyes and shrugged jerkily, forcing the images of dead soldiers aside.

Zane nodded in the pastor's direction. "What's he saying?"

"War," Pastor Cavanaugh grumbled, "Always war." He glanced at the pulpit. A sculptured Christ stared back with saddened eyes. "Lord, how long am I forced to see you this way? I know the Catholics brought you here in good faith after their church roof collapsed but with supplies running low, buildings being destroyed and thousands homeless, what has happened to the priorities of man? Have we all gone insane? And now I must endure your likeness." He suddenly huffed. "At least I can focus my frustrations.

109

But I'm too old for this. My heart is heavy, weak. Lord, how many wars do we have to suffer before you come back? You have taught me much but I am encumbered by a world in anguish. My faith needs emendation." He then stooped and coughed. "What faith?"

A blue light flashed across the vaulted beamed ceiling, the wooden arches trailing their shadows across the walls. Cavanaugh glanced up as the light added a tinge of blue around the candle flames. He turned away, not seeming to care until a blast of frigid air burst apart the door that led to the cellar and catacombs, a gush of wind punching him to the ground. The heavy statue of Christ rocked on its pedestal, the stained glass behind creaking as it bowed from the push of air. The old oak door now hung awkwardly on one hinge.

"I've done it!" cried a hollow, distant voice. A girl raced up from the cellar, her footsteps echoing louder but slowing in pace until she stopped to quickly examine the damaged door. Then she noticed her father sprawled on the floor, struggling to sit up.

"Papa!"

"Niva!" he barked. "The time has come to stop your experiments. If the senior district pastor ever finds out about this…"

"Papa, I'm so sorry," she wailed, her voice tense as she helped her elderly father to his feet. "But the experiment," she paused, catching her breath, "it works... it really works."

"No buts," her father said firmly. "I have been too accommodating of your talents. It's got to stop." He frowned at her and touched her fringe, as if disapproving of the blonde streaks she wore at either side of her otherwise black straight hair. He looked up and down at her tall slender frame as if he hadn't realized how fast she had grown. "You need to fill out dear," he said sternly. "Those tight jeans make your legs look like tooth picks. You spend too much time down there in the catacombs; you need to eat. And you need to stop those crazy experiments."

"It *will* stop," Niva insisted, brushing her hair aside. "I no longer need to test the loculus. It works."

Pastor Cavanaugh glanced back at the statue of Christ, and then looked more closely, his eyes glazed with curiosity. "Lord, you look almost quizzical, not sad at all."

"Oh Papa, stop looking at that thing. Can't we put it somewhere else?

"We have a shared congregation now, dear. Times are desperate and this is God's house to all.

"But hardly anyone comes now," she insisted.

He rubbed his chin and eyed Niva carefully. "Put aside your concerns about the unwanted statue. Now tell me about that old equipment. It really works?"

"Yes," she breathed.

He sighed. "Why couldn't you just leave the boys to their science? Then we wouldn't have that mess down there, which incidentally, I thought you were going to remove from the unused crypts." He sighed again. "If only you had grown up to like horses or netball or something girls like."

"Oh Papa, I'm sorry I'm not the person you wanted me to be. I scare you, and you know it—"

"No, no child," he said softly, shaking his head.

"It's true. I can't help being five years ahead of my own year in school. I can't help it if quantum physics is as easy as playing chess and I can't help it if boys are scared of me."

He broke with a smile and embraced her. "Ah, you're so special and I do so love you very much. Mama would be proud."

Niva produced a comb and sat her father down on one of the pews. She began to brush his wiry hair, ignoring her own wind-swept appearance. "You don't mind then?"

"Of course not, dear. I place great faith in you, no matter how much your endeavors seem misguided or pointless."

Niva took his hand and squeezed gently. "Not misguided," she said softly. "The loculus works. It really works and I think I even surprised myself."

"What's she talking about?" Zane asked.

"Something to do with that light and wind," Angela replied. "When it came, I felt a tingling sensation all over."

"Me too," Zane said. "Let's go through that busted door and see what's down in their basement."

Cavanaugh frowned and folded his arms. "Oh Niva, you really believe so? You have achieved so much ... but something written in a book by Wells?"

"Look," Niva said firmly, "Proof is here." She fumbled in her pocket and produced a cell phone. She tapped the screen and dragged her finger to scroll through a set of images. "Now you know this phone has a built in camera with self-timer and date stamp."

"Err, yes... but—"

"Look at the picture of this church."

Cavanaugh took the phone and examined the picture. He scratched his head. "What am I supposed to look at? It's our church, our little ancient stone church. A touristy bucolic building that gets more

113

tourists on a weekend than a congregation at Easter. What of it?"

"Look," Niva insisted.

Pastor Cavanaugh rubbed the bristling gray hairs on his chin as he examined the image. The surrounding trees appeared different.

"Look at the conifer," she said.

Pastor Cavanaugh wrinkled his brow in thought.

"See?" she said excitedly, "That old conifer outside the window. That hasn't been next to this church for five years. *Five years*."

"Destroyed in a storm," Cavanaugh mumbled slowly. "So it's..." – he sat upright and looked her carefully in the eyes – "an old photo then. You scanned an old photo into the phone. I know they have scanners built into some phones these days. I'm not an old fool, you know."

"Oh Papa, don't be so obtuse." she whisked the phone off him and began tapping again. "I'm not a liar," she said quietly, her eyes scanning the screen.

"Niva," he said tersely.

"Sorry, Papa, but please look at the time and date stamp. It doesn't lie." She thrust the phone before him. "This image was taken not half an hour ago and that tree hasn't been there for five years."

He shook his head slowly. "But it can't be..."

She dropped the cell phone into her lap. "Oh, why don't you believe? I set the self-timer for two minutes, placed it onto the grid in the mini-test unit and put the whole thing outside. When the power loculus activated, the cell phone disappeared, followed by the loculus itself in *transattach* mode. Auto recall brought the loculus and its contents back to the pre-configured coordinates, inside my test lab.

"Well," Cavanaugh said, rubbing the back of his neck, "It's all over my head. But something did push me to the ground..." He stood up and rubbed his graying whiskers again. He slowly paced the church, not saying a word, and glanced at the statue of Christ through the corners of his eyes. He swung to his daughter and snapped his fingers. "For the love of... I don't know what... Wanting to believe? Show me how this... this loculus works."

Niva's eyes lit with excitement. "Papa, I promise I have put the unused crypt to good use. You haven't been there for a long time. It's a little untidy and there are cables everywhere and—"

"Hush, child," he said softly, "so long as you didn't throw out my old collection of vintage labels..." He coughed and winked, adding, "for communion service, of course."

115

"But… I – I had to move everything," she blurted, "because I've built a bigger loculus, built to hold two."

Her father shrank back, dumbfounded. "How? How could I not know this?"

"You are so busy with your parish. You never seemed interested in my work." She gripped his arm and swung for the partly-wrenched door that led to the cellar. "But now," she said, beaming, "now that I have something to prove, I have my father's interest again, yes?"

"We shall see," he said dryly. "I've been a little nervous about going down there, especially since you inherited all that old equipment from Uncle Jürgen."

"Come, I'll show you," she said and motioned.

He followed her down the narrow stone steps leading to the cellar. "I know some of the Aramaic languages and I can speak Hebrew," he said confidently, "some Greek and Latin—"

"Huh?" she asked, half listening.

"Oh, idle thoughts my child, idle thoughts."

9: Return to the Truth

"Co-o-o-l!"

Zane stretched the word from his lips as he gazed around the cellar. "What a load of crap this is. Wish Dad had a basement like this; it's great."

"Well, is it good or is it bad?" Angela asked with frustration.

"It's good shit." Zane looked around and raised his glowing arms. "Just look at it all..."

"Bit like Dad's lab," Angela said, "but really untidy."

They hovered around the cellar, their little glows seemingly bouncing off shiny metal fascia plates covered in knobs and dials from equipment mounted in metal rack cabinets. Hundreds of lights flickered in the semi-light. Zane noticed a small black box on a pedestal, open at the top with a grid at its base. Several red and blue cables stretched away from it like arteries.

"Here they come," Angela said, grabbing his arm.

"My my, you've been busy," Pastor Cavanaugh said as he entered the cellar. "Feels like I've walked into a 1950s sci-fi movie set."

117

"Oh, please," Niva laughed. "Some of this stuff may be old but I have put a lot of it to good use, even the old chronometers that have nixie tubes; they all still work and don't suffer from intense electrical field disturbance."

"I see," her father breathed. "But every wall is covered. I can't spot a bare stone anywhere. At least you didn't block that little window to the outside world." He pointed, before huffing with amazement. "I didn't know Professor Jürgen had so much junk!"

"Everything from tube to surface mount, which I need to shield," Niva said.

Pastor Cavanaugh surveyed the large cellar. Walls were dressed in rows of rack cabinets filled with instrumentation that blinked in unison, all linked by heavy cables snaking across the stone floor, only elevated in areas where chunky chrome junctions met in the web of wires. He stepped awkwardly through the gaps, thinking he was in a kind of forest knotted with tree roots. Banks of heavy computer drives sat like old telephone boxes next to small cases mounted with digital displays, flickering row upon row of red status lights. In the half light, Pastor Cavanaugh stood amidst the clicking, whirring and droning; a fleeting thought crossed his mind that all of this was alive somehow.

Something hummed in the room beyond. Through a partly-open door, Cavanaugh spotted a momentary trickle of soft yellow light against the mossy stone wall. He peered inside and blinked as the light returned to fill the otherwise dimly-lit room. He could barely make out a gray outline, a large black silhouette filling the room. The light came from underneath, giving no illumination to the blackness above it. He approached the shape and saw that it was like a large black box raised above a grid on the floor.

"What's this, Niva? It's bigger than a garage. How on earth did you get this in here?"

"Full size version of the mini time loculus," Niva said proudly. "It's a perfect cube. In it we can go anywhere and anywhen."

"Anywhen? How quaint, Miss Einstein!"

Niva rolled her eyes. "Would you like me to explain the theory, the quantum dynamics and Q-values that went into this device?"

"Ahem, another time, my dear," he said flatly.

"Yes, it's not an easy thing to explain to the ordinary person." She bit her lip. "Not that you're an ordinary person, Papa," she said and smiled.

He glanced at some of the bench equipment hooked up to a series of cables that led to the loculus. Most of it was built into heavy metal cases. "Guess you won't have a problem with EMR?" he asked, raising his brows.

"Smart ass," she laughed. "Yes, it's quite directional in this configuration. The other day an electromagnetic burst from the loculus ruined the neighbor's television."

"Ah yes," Pastor Cavanaugh nodded and said, "On a Sunday. That would explain why my public address amplifier near the pulpit died mid-service."

"Oh, no you don't," Niva said carefully. "You know I don't work here when you do your services."

"Of course, dear, and I wouldn't worry about losing my television in the vestry either, what with all this war going on. Who needs it?" He stared blankly at the loculus looming in the dark, a moment of yellow light slowly emanating from beneath the raised portion. Its glow swelled and faded like a heartbeat, accompanied by a soft droning sound with each reach of light.

And then an instance of weariness reached his eyes and he tilted his head slightly.

"Okay, Papa?"

"Yes," he said softly. He coughed and steadied himself. "So how does one get inside? I can't see a door."

"With this," Niva said as she aimed what looked like a garage door remote control at the loculus.

The once smooth-facing wall now etched into the surface a door frame which then dropped back slightly and quietly slid open to reveal a soft glow of colored instrument lamps and computer monitors inside.

Her father shook his head in disbelief. "Just how on earth did you create this thing?"

"Same particle manipulation I learned from Jürgen's theories. He worked with Professor Tipler you know. Jürgen said matter can be manipulated in much the same way scientists manipulate genes, only it's a density equivalent given to a precise mathematical structure that allows solidity to be re-defined and scaled from below an atomic level—"

Her father hushed her. "Okay," he said, "I am impressed with what you have done with the inheritance from Professor Jürgen. You must have received quite a fortune; I was, well, too modest to ask how much."

"A lot," Niva said firmly. "I am a very lucky girl. I know scientists out there who would kill for the kind of funding I have available."

"But such a gamble," he said. "It could have all been for nothing."

"Faith," Niva said. "Isn't that what you always told me? Money only goes so far. Faith and works also help."

Her father looked down. "Wish my faith was so steadfast," he mumbled.

Angela watched with a curious look in her eyes as Pastor Cavanaugh and Niva discussed the essence of time travel, something her father once mentioned after reading a magazine article about a discovery where micro particles are shifted back in time by a few seconds.

Zane did not appear so interested. Instead he gazed through the tiny stone window near the basement ceiling. It was ground level outside and a moon had just appeared over the horizon. He wanted to go home. He didn't care much for this crazy trip through death, about passing through domains of the living and the dead, of dead soldiers without their ghosts and dead people walking around a world like his own where nobody could see him, except Mister Abaddon.

A shiver rippled through his ghostly spine and he turned away. So far the voice had not returned and he swung to face Angela, almost stupefied by the blinking lights of this strange room. "Where do you think we are?"

"Huh? Oh, I don't know," Angela said. "Maybe we're in Europe somewhere, given that funny church name. What's it matter?"

"They speak English," Zane said. "Weird, huh?"

"Maybe it's because of all the British troops and bases here. I saw something on the notice board out there about allies and support."

"But they're alone here, except for us," Zane said.

"Well, the pastor sounds British, but his daughter sounds German. And the congregation is diverse, too," Angela said. "But, you know, sometimes I feel I can sense the thoughts behind the words, before the words are said. And sometimes I feel a different thought behind a word, like a contradictory thought."

"What?" Zane asked, scrunching his face. "That doesn't make sense."

Angela shrugged and smiled awkwardly.

"People just get around," Zane said. "Like we do. We could be anywhere. When I think about it, we've certainly traveled, of a sort. Those funnels must be like wormholes, after all, well mini-ones at that."

"You think?" Angela said with slight derision.

"How else do you explain it?"

Angela rolled her eyes.

Zane hovered to the loculus, brushing past the old pastor who stood near the entrance.

Pastor Cavanaugh shuddered and then looked down despondently.

Niva took his arms and tried to hold his heavy hands together inside hers. "I love you, Papa. I have faith in you. You have it too..." She opened his hand and pressed his weighty palm against his heart. "You must find it in the many rooms in there."

Her father looked up and forced a smile. "Take me back."

Niva gave him a puzzled look. "Back? Back where?"

"To the time of Christ."

"Christ?"

"Now now, don't take his name in vain—"

"Silly," she said and folded her arms. "I mean, you want to go back that far?"

"Yes!" He clapped his hands, and looked up at her with anticipation.

Niva paced the uneven floor. "I don't know," she said doubtfully. "This is all new. It's too risky. I have to make grid calculations, latitude and longitude and so on. It's—"

Something rumbled outside, the subtle tremor reaching beneath their shoes.

"What was that?"

Her father gave a momentary sideways glance and gripped her shoulders, staring evenly into her eyes. "I need to know. If *He* won't come to us, then we'll go to *Him*."

"Then you *do* believe," Niva said.

Pastor Cavanaugh breathed heavily. "I... I don't know anymore. But don't you see? We now have the means to travel back in time to discover if Jesus is who he says he is. We all know he existed as an historical figure but what of God? What if he really is the son of God?"

"Now you doubt."

"Yes, Niva," he sighed. He glanced at the open door to the loculus which seemed to beckon him. He released his grip on Niva's shoulders and stepped into the loculus.

"Wait, Papa."

"Amazing, Niva, truly amazing." He sat on an old swivel chair and surveyed the panel controls. "I won't touch a thing, promise. Now where have I seen these chairs before?"

Niva followed him into the loculus. She glanced to one side and removed a photo of a young woman pinned to the wall above her main computer monitor.

Zane flitted past her to look at the photo and thought how the lady looked similar to his own mother, long dark hair slightly curled, her hazel eyes open wide and a broad smile.

"Ah," Pastor Cavanaugh said and clapped his hands, "faith and works as Saint James tells us. This is a shining example," he said as he scanned the controls.

The myriad of panel lights cast a glow across the pastor's eyes and they seemed to spell out letters. He mumbled the characters as he fell into a kind of trance. A shadow swept past the lights.

Opening his eyes he sprang upright and said in a demanding tone, "Who's in here?"

"Angela, he saw me... Angela?"

"Shush, Zane, I'm right behind you."

"The priest saw me!"

Angela rolled her eyes and Zane caught a mocking glint. "Not again," she said. "He's not a priest; he's a pastor. And he can't see you."

"Sorry, just panicking but I feel, when I move, people can see me."

Angela folded her arms. "We're not in Hell, there's no Mister Abaddon and the Dumpster Man says nobody can see you."

"Who is this dumpster guy, anyway?" Zane floated backwards and swayed his head from side to side, grinning, his hands outstretched. "Dumpster Man," – he wiggled his fingers before her –"Woooh..."

Angela huffed and feathered towards Niva who was adjusting some dials on the largest control panel which sloped away from the wall.

"Papa, there's no one else in here with us," Niva said. "You're being silly. There's a lot going on with this device and a big field to generate and I need to concentrate. Maybe... maybe you won't be able to cope with time travel."

"I can cope," he huffed. "I'm just a little tired of the world," – he waved his hands in the air – "*this* world." He struggled to his feet. "I simply need to find out—"

An explosion rippled outside, a whoosh of air shrilling past and shattering the narrow window in the cellar. Pastor Cavanaugh lunged out of the Loculus and raced up the stony stairs leading to the old church. Forgetting the strain in his back, he heaved the heavy oak door aside without care; it came unhinged completely, falling against the wall with a clattering, splintered wood echo that rang down the corridor to the crypts below.

He crossed the floor to the main church doors and flung them open to stare blindly into a now calm night sky. Two silhouettes streaked past. Two bats, he thought. A moment of silence passed but for a few crickets, until a riveting crackle of thunder caused him to duck and cover his ears. Fire trails lit the sky. He looked back into the church as the fire trails painted a swirling brushstroke of light upon the old stained glass in almost hypnotic motions.

"Papa, come back!" Niva's voice reverberated from below. "Come back down here, quickly."

Pastor Cavanaugh stood frozen, aghast at the closing firestorm. His shoes felt bolted to the ground but he managed to wrench himself free from the shock to dash for the cellar. He rightly guessed what was happening and he knew it would be here fast.

The expanse of stained glass groaned and heaved inwards before shattering from the push of atmosphere that had the stench of fuel. A fire trail followed the fuel vapors as white bursting veins of heat smothered every corner of the church. The statue of Jesus skipped off the pedestal and crashed to scorched parquetry in a shower of glass and rubble.

A talon of fire licked at Pastor Cavanaugh's robes as he dashed down the ancient steps to the cellar where he slipped on the smoothed stone, falling to bite the cold floor.

Niva slammed the weighty cellar door behind him, latching all three bolts. Fire licked through the cracks, slowly receding as the flames abated.

"Niva... that shockwave—"

"Door is shut, Papa. Here!" She struggled to lift him up, gasping for air as a swirl of smoke streamed through the broken window.

"I'm okay, dear," he said, as they stumbled into the loculus. "One of those ... fuel-air bombs." Her father groaned as he fell onto the loculus floor. "The war is here."

"We've got to leave now, for sure," Niva said, bending over her father. "This'll be our first trip." She touched his singed hair where it had coiled from the heat. "You were lucky."

Her father casually waved his hand. "Don't fuss over me child. Just get us out of here."

Niva looked at him with a fleeting glance of fear. "You know, we could start a cause and effect chain that'll ripple through the centuries."

"So long as the years don't kill as many people; so long as I don't get back here to find myself in this decrepit state."

"I'm not going out there, Ange," Zane said. "You must be mad."

"Zane, no harm can come to us," Angela insisted. "I just want to know what's going on outside."

"Isn't it obvious? The empty death we passed back there on the hillside has caught up with us here. I don't understand the funnel that brought us here. It was a light one but this place is no picnic. Didn't you say a dark funnel goes to a scary place? Go figure."

Angela shook her head and then shrugged, confused by the funnel herself. "Never been like that before. Thought I could rely on them but I suppose we can't trust the density and light of a funnel anymore. Maybe it's because you're with me; it gets all confused or something."

"Me?" Zane said dumbfounded, "What have I got to do with it? Maybe we just can't tell what's bad and what's not anymore." He scratched his head and rolled his eyes, "But that's the dumbest thing I could say."

"Don't know anymore," Angela said, shaking her head. "But your presence has kind of affected things. I feel it. Anyway, I'd like to get away from here. Let's just peek outside to see if a funnel's nearby."

"You do it. Besides, I want to see if this piece of junk works."

"If it does, chances are it won't take us with them," Angela said. "We're ghosts, remember? We can't be moved by fast-moving physical things."

"But Numan's car moved us." Zane waved his glowing arms in the air. "Just maybe this loculus thingy will too."

"Depends," she said slowly. "That was a funny place. Gee, I wish I knew about quantum physics like Niva, but maybe you're right for once, Zane."

"For once?" he said with a grimaced.

"Funnel or no funnel, Zane, I guess right now the loculus could be our best chance to leave this place. No matter how harmless to us that war is out there, I really don't want the mental torture of it."

A screeching rippled through the church grounds. The heavy cellar beams creaked from a pressure above.

"Church is collapsing," Niva shrieked, as she cranked a lever on the wall.

Pastor Cavanaugh glanced through the open loculus door as the ceiling jutted inwards then tore open, the statue of Christ crashing through to land almost upright in a pile of rubble on the crypt floor.

Niva flicked a panel switch and the door to the cube hissed and slid shut. The edges then melded together, the door becoming part of the wall again. "Hermetically sealed to quantum level," she said to her father, who looked on with shock and awe.

Her father glanced beyond a central column, following Niva's actions on the control panel. Two old leather chairs sat bolted to the floor grid. Niva sat on one and flicked up an array of switches.

"I'm so proud of you, Niva... so proud."

131

"Gotta leave now," she said quickly. She tapped an old brass gauge. "Ceiling's about to cave in from debris above." She rotated a dial attached to a digital display which began to scroll a sequence of numbers. "Uh-oh, not much energy in store; the cyclotron is pushed."

"Energy? Where do you get that from, anyway?"

"Long story, Papa." She smiled quickly. "The thorium reactor's power-to-mass ratio never quite added up in the computer simulation, but I always seemed to have enough liquid energy for displacement and I still can't understand why. The draw from the small reactor goes beyond its lifter capacity when operational, as if tapped from another source and I'm sure in-flight self-generation has something to do with it – almost a complementary fusion effect but I don't know why. However, we still may not have enough juice to get us back, depending on the initial energy utilization to get us out of here in the first place. It seems to vary with each experiment, very strange."

Pastor Cavanaugh breathed heavily. "Get us back to what?" His head fell back on the cold floor of the loculus.

"Silly me," Niva said. She stood up and removed her cardigan, folding it into a pillow and placing it under her father's head. "Relax as best you can there, dear Papa. There should be no internal movement, only external, so you don't need to worry about strapping in." She wiped his brow with a handkerchief and then returned to the console.

Another rafter groaned under the pressure above the loculus.

"Now," her father breathed. "Now!"

The grid on the floor underneath him began to glow as Niva tugged a lever. "These old signal levers are heavy," she panted. "There should be little disorientation. If you feel it, it'll only last a moment. The outside will spin like a gyro but in here we'll barely notice it."

"Glad to hear it," he said with a cough.

"An internal-external displacement occurs which creates a field that encapsulates anything within preconfigured parameters."

"Okay, dear," he sighed, waving his hand and knowing it was all beyond his comprehension. "My feet are tingling."

The outer hull of the loculus spun faster and faster, flinging away the debris that had already landed on it.

Zane and Angela clung tightly to what essence of the central column they could feel, merging themselves into what felt like the most stable material.

Losing her grip, Angela began to drift away from the column until Zane yanked her back.

"This-s-s-s-s is-s-s-s-s the cr-r-raziest d-death one g-g-ghost coul-l-ld pos-s-s-sibly h-ha-a-a-ve," Zane buzzed.

Angela didn't reply and Zane gave up on the next sentence he was about to say – about traveling without the aid of a funnel. It didn't really matter. All he wanted to do was make it to wherever in one piece. He thought how ridiculous that sounded but when he looked into Angela's dark greenish eyes, he knew she felt it too. A wrenching sensation made him feel like something was attempting to disperse him or put his spirit through a sieve. It was unnerving and he wondered how long it would last.

Outside, the spinning loculus began to disappear, the ruination of the church above giving way and falling to the ground as the time cube uttered a ruptured echo. In a flash of golden light the time cube then vanished, signaling their departure.

10: Jesus Freak

The loculus shrilled through a sky blue void shredded in luminous vapors.

Pastor Cavanaugh lay on the glowing floor until a sudden loss of gravity threw him towards the chairs. Niva stretched out her arms and clutched his robes, dragging him into the seat beside her. "Sorry," she yelled, "I wasn't counting on midflight stability fluctuations. Better strap in after all. Glad I put these in!"

The loculus juddered as he attempted to speak. "Chairs ... f-f-from vestry. You... you must ask and th-thou sh-shalt be-be gi-v-v-en."

"Sor-ry." She glanced at a panel meter as the vibrating decreased. A row of digital displays rapidly ticked back their calendar sequences until finally slowing.

"Almost there... and *then.*"

With a crackling thunder, the loculus materialized just above a rocky surface, decelerating to finally drop with a deadening thud, the cube tilting slightly in a haze of dust.

"What a landing!" Niva puffed. "Papa, you okay?"

"Quite okay, dear, just a little dizzy."

"That'll pass." She examined the readouts. "Now, according to lunar calculations and calendar sequence we should be... good God!"

Pastor Cavanaugh leaned forward, his pallid face full of concern. "What, child?"

Niva's face was red. "We have only three days to find Jesus. Just three days before he's crucified!"

Her father slumped back in his chair. "Are we near Jerusalem?"

Niva tapped some buttons. "Not sure. I think we're a long way from there."

Her father sighed. "He'll be in Jerusalem by now." He raised his hands to a ceiling draped in a parachute of wires and cables. "Lord, so close. But where in the Twelve Tribes are we?" He gulped and looked at Niva with a forlorn expression on his face. "Can we go back further?"

"No chance, no energy. We need to recharge."

Her father unbuckled himself from the chair and stood up. "Can we have a look outside?"

"Yes," Niva said and sniffed. She switched on a small monitor.

"Good Lord," he said. "Desert. Could stretch for miles for all we know." He fiddled with a joystick control and figured it to be a camera angle controller. "Wow, zillions of stars. We could be anywhere..."

The loculus door hissed open and Niva dashed outside.

"Where are you going?" he yelled after her. "There could be dangers in the night." He stumbled out of the loculus onto the uneven ground to face a night that was brisk and still.

Zane eyed Angela and she shrugged.

Niva stood in a sandy rock-strewn area in the distance, looking up to the sky. The air smelt salty and her father coughed from the settling dust kicked up into the air by the cube's arrival. He approached her carefully, almost expecting her to run from him. He knew something was wrong and he knew it was somehow his fault.

She swung about, her face streaming in tears. "Do you realize," she blurted, "I could have seen a mother I hardly knew?"

Her father looked down. He dug his hands deep into his pockets and kicked a stone. "The cost, I ... I should have known."

He looked back at her standing there alone, now more distant from him than the few yards they were apart.

A soft breeze toyed with her hair and he took a step towards her.

She stepped back and stopped abruptly, then wiping the tears from her eyes, she approached him hesitantly.

"Niva?" he said softly.

He reached for her and pulled her into his arms, holding her close and drawing back to look down into her lost eyes.

"Dear child, I am so sorry. I've been a stupid, selfish old man. How could I not realize your burning desire to see Mama again? I am such a fool. The time machine, all your endless work on what I thought was junk. How stupid could I be? Susan... she was so beautiful, just like you are now." He held her close and gazed into her eyes. "She is in you, Niva. She is very much a part of you."

"Papa, I always prayed for you to hold her again."

"I know, I know," he said as he scratched the corner of his eye.

Niva smiled slightly at her father's uncertain gaze. She looked into his eyes and nodded slowly.

Her father suddenly grinned, as if he had produced this change in her. He wiped a salt trail off her cheek.

"Papa, we're here now. Let's just track down the main man."

Pastor Cavanaugh took his daughter's hand as they ambled back to the loculus, the tiny light from the entrance guiding their way in a black and endless desert.

"We have much to do," her father said. "Adjust our appearances, tackle possible encounters with Romans, try to speak the local tongue."

"You can speak Hebrew, Greek and Latin, Papa. I can only speak German and English, which I don't think will help here," she said with a cautious grin.

"Don't worry, my dear. Let me do the talking. But we should make haste while it's dark."

"Why?"

"Well, firstly, it's more comfortable to travel at night. This area is semi-arid but we must be near the sea somewhere." He sniffed. "The air is a bit salty. We'll also have to obtain some proper clothing."

Niva gave a quizzical and slightly suspicious look. "Obtain?"

"Alright, then," he groaned. "Steal." He looked skywards. "Lord forgive us for what we are about to do."

Niva entered the loculus and sat down to examine a computer estimate of their surroundings. "We seem to be roughly four or so miles east of the Mediterranean Sea, probably near the Port of Sidon or Tyre, if these archive readings correspond to current geography." She looked up at her father's concerned face. "Can you cope with the walk?"

He nodded slowly and smiled. "After traveling two thousand years, what's in a few miles?"

"Wonder what that's all about, out there?" Zane motioned with his thumb.

"It's not our business," Angela replied flatly. "Niva's upset at Daddy and that's that. They seem okay now."

"Can't believe we actually moved with them in time," Zane said. "I almost expect to see a road nearby and some big lights from heavy trucks in the night."

Angela hovered over to Zane who mused over the controls. "The Dumpster Man never mentioned time travel, or weird worlds like Numan's."

Zane rolled his eyes. "When we goin' to meet this dude? Where is he and how'd you meet him?"

"So, you're interested now?"

"I always was!" Zane protested.

Angela swallowed and stared into the blackness outside the loculus. "It was just after I died—"

"Yeah, you never did answer that question. So how'd you..."

"Die?" Angela shuddered. "Like you, I don't remember much. A few weeks after the explosion at Dad's factory there was a power failure. Mom had already gone out to get groceries and hadn't returned and I wanted to phone her to bring some milk, as the old milk was getting stinky. The power was down on our side of the street. The phones weren't working either. I just remember a big bright light while running across the road to see Cath, my neighbor. It was dark and something hit me severe."

"A car?"

"Only saw one light, unless the other didn't work and it sure wasn't a motorbike. That thump really got me ... but the lights, they were so bright, and I felt a burning all over.

"You said only one light."

"They came after..." she paused, "after the thump. That's all I remember. The Dumpster Man says there's a shock period that every spirit has before waking in the spirit realm. Some wake up quicker than others. Some don't quite wake up completely, just hover like

141

zombie ghosts. Some don't wake up at all. I think I got my wakeup call when my body was cremated. Thought I had woken up in Hell for a moment, until I realized I was in some kind of heat chamber with all these bursts of flames and smoke. I freaked out; I shot through the side of the place and found myself outside a funeral home to watch my mother bawling her eyes out over me. I felt so sorry for her, but you know, as a ghost I was lucky. Some ghosts who wake up don't want to move on. They want to stay where they died or go back to their homes and hover in loneliness, until something—"

"Our cat got run over by a car," Zane said.

"What?" she looked at him oddly.

"No serious – injured and bleeding it staggered back to Mom and climbed onto her lap, where it died in her arms. It was the only safe place it knew. Maybe home is the only place a ghost has."

"But they're the ones who are taken – and when they least expect it. It happened to a friend ghost."

"Taken? By what – a reaper?"

"The Dumpster Man calls them Munchers—"

"Sure," Zane said disbelievingly. "Quit it with this guy. What's he know, anyway?"

"He's been around death a lot longer than you or I. I trust him... sort of."

Zane shrugged. "Okay, what would I know? Sorry." He offered a slight smile which lifted his tired eyes. "I'm beginning to trust you."

Angela returned a flicker of a smile.

"So your dad—"

"He must have died in the explosion, but there was no trace," she cut in quickly.

"Sorry."

Angela sighed. "Doesn't matter now. Mom wanted to put off his funeral, saying that he may suddenly turn up with that pony he promised, like the ones he used to ride – just to keep me guessing, I suppose. But she knew he was gone and deep down I knew too. The police found the partial remains of a lab assistant. His body was not so blown, they said – more like sliced in pieces; only the upper bits were there, the head, shoulders and—"

"Gross," Zane muttered.

"A lot of the factory lab was gone too, almost like it disappeared rather than exploded, as there wasn't much rubble. There was a big crater where it used to stand." She gave a long sigh. "We eventually had the funeral. A week later it was my turn to die; God knows the reason, if there is one, and now, even as a ghost, I couldn't find Dad anywhere. When I first ran into the

Dumpster Man he assured me Dad was okay but he wouldn't give me any specifics."

"Maybe he doesn't know everything," Zane remarked.

"Or tell perhaps. Don't know why I believed him that Dad's just fine," she continued, "but I'd believe anything then. I hung around Mom for as long as I could, but she never talked about the accident to anyone. I also hung around the other scientists to listen in and find out more about the explosion but they didn't say much either. When alive, I'd been to the lab and seen the cyclotron but I still didn't understand what went on and there was always a guard watching us. After I died, I came back to look down the several levels where the cyclotron was, but it was gone too. No one can explain it."

"Cyclotron?"

"Atomic reactor. Dad said it was used to generate the artificial Kirlian force fields."

"Uh-huh." Zane nodded distractedly. "Sorry about your dad. Your mom must feel like crap right now."

"Sure, if you like." She frowned slightly. "She'll nurse a pain for the rest of her life. The Dumpster Man told me if Mom doesn't change her thinking and stop blaming herself for my death, she'll be trapped by her own conscience after she dies, whatever that—" her eyes suddenly bulged and she looked upwards.

"What?"

"Just like Numan ... Why didn't I understand it before?"

"Well, you sort of did," Zane started, tilting his head. "Like he created his own hell, you know, like Hell isn't just a bad place for no-gooders, but more what you make it."

"But it's more than that, what with all those other dead dudes sharing the same hell."

"A place for similar-minded people?" Zane asked.

"Maybe," she said, touching her chin, her wide eyes staring into space with curiosity. "Maybe Dad's in his own hell, but that doesn't make sense. He was always happy and kind. The Dumpster Man's not telling me the whole story."

"Where's he hang out, this Dumpster dude?"

"In an industrial dump yard near Dad's factory. There's an old car scrap yard there too."

Zane whacked his forehead. "Duh, a dump yard; go figure."

"He's kinda rough-looking, not much hair on top, with a big fat, almost permanently grinning face and a fat body to go with it, with daggy greasy denim overalls … and there're always bits of wire hanging out of his pockets, old chains, broken cell phones, calculators and pens. I met him not long after I died, while hanging around the factory after the explosion. The police had surrounded everything with ribbons, like it was a crime scene."

"Maybe it was," Zane said suspiciously.

"I don't know." She offered a glum look and wide, lost eyes. "I'll probably never know. Anyway, all the press had gone and I saw this funny trash man inspecting junk at the back of the factory. Dad used to lob all kinds of stuff into the bin, like reject components for industrial timers and temperature-sensing gadgets. Then I caught the Dumpster Man staring straight at me from a distance, as I watched from a torn-away window near the blown-up part of the factory. I couldn't figure how he saw me, and then guessed he was dead like me. It was hard to tell with all that junk hanging out of his clothes, and then I realized it was his own ghostly self-projection, like we have of ourselves – you know, how we look, like our faces don't change and we keep our own clothes on as ghosts."

"Yeah, come to think of it," Zane said then paused. "So what we're wearing is a perception or memory of what we wore when alive, maybe what we think of as being comfortable about ourselves. That'd explain why I look different from the way my body was dressed in my coffin, with those stinkin' best clothes. I wonder…"

"Yes, Zane, and I wondered about changing my default ghostly clothes. But when I try to think of something in my closet to wear, it doesn't come on."

"Maybe we gotta think harder."

"Tried that."

"Well maybe Dumpster Dude can give you a pointer or two," Zane said.

"Maybe," she replied. "I get an unsettling feeling when I think about him. I'm sure he's essentially a good ghost, but there is a lot more to this guy and I just can't put my phantom finger on it."

Zane watched her face go blank, her eyes still wide open, as if they were gazing right through him to another space; her face glowed from a certain kind of fear and sadness.

"You think the afterlife is spooky?" she asked. "I had enough trouble with the living world. Dad worked so hard and, although everyone said how nice a guy he is, I didn't get to see him much. Mom got the heebies every time I complained. She was probably under a lot of stress over mortgages, bills and so on. Scientists don't get paid that much, you know, but they carry the world's future on their shoulders. Mom worked as a

147

lab assistant for another company and earned even less money. Yet they still insisted on putting me through the best school, which was not a very nice school anyway – full of pompous upstarts and, unfortunately, my lack of appreciation probably showed."

"I'm sorry your Mom blames herself," Zane said quietly. He tried to think back to his own death and wondered why he wasn't burned to ash like almost everyone else these days. A hint of memory ran up the back of his neck and he looked up at Angela with curiosity. "Hey, what you said about burning when you died; I felt that too. Didn't you say you were cremated?"

"Yes, but I remember the burning happening at the point of my death, not after, but that's all I remember. I didn't actually feel anything when I woke in the furnace. I had already dashed outside and I couldn't really face looking at my own body being reduced to fit into a canister."

"Well, as you know, I wasn't cremated," Zane said. "Yet, when you mention it, I felt that burning sensation too. Wonder why?"

"Oh, I don't know," Angela said with a quiet sigh. "Look Zane, our hosts are leaving. Enough morbid talk; let's follow these guys."

***

A flat sheet of sea mirrored the edge of the descending moon, the crystal waters broken by the dark gray shapes of a town jutting above the horizon, their edges slightly tinged in orange by the onset of morning. The air was warm already, a little humid but not sultry. Pastor Cavanaugh and his daughter had already passed through the slopes of a vineyard, pausing to remove some forgotten clothes left out to dry.

"We narrowly escaped that wiry old man," he said.

"What was he yelling at us?"

"You wouldn't want to know, Niva," he said flatly. "Let's just say, apart from one or two words I couldn't pick up, it weren't pleasant."

"Talk about thieves in the night," Niva laughed.

"I'm not amused," her father said, breaking into a chuckle. "Well, we'll drop these back when we're finished. Look, it's almost light."

Niva yawned. "We had a short and rocky sleep back there. What I'd give for a soft bed."

Pastor Cavanaugh examined his acquired clothing in the morning light, a purple robe draped over his ministerial garb. "Hmm, this is well made, complete with tassels and decorative borders. Pleasantly warm too."

Niva pirouetted in her blue flax tunic which covered her jeans down to her ankles. "I think we shall blend in nicely, Papa."

"Maybe," he said dryly. "But these are the robes of rich folk. And I don't think the bleaches in your hair are fitting."

"Maybe," she said with a huff, offering a slight smile a moment later.

"Rich and careless people," her father continued. "Fancy leaving this on the ground nearby." He reached for a small pouch attached to his belt and produced a handful of silver coins. "I think we're in Tyre. This is Greek currency, drachmas freshly minted. They might even mint them here. We're lucky to have these."

"Glad you prepared for this," she said flatly.

A passing woman with head pad and jar had stopped to listen to their English tones. Pastor Cavanaugh instantly motioned for Niva to detour and follow. Both walked briskly down the rocky street leading to the port.

"Just let me do the talking, Niva," he whispered. "We must find a way to get to Jerusalem. Hopefully we'll be able to board a boat for Joppa then head inland." He lifted his tunic and grinned. "Time to gird up our loins."

"Look!" Niva said.

They spotted a crowd heading towards the beach near the sea port. Cavanaugh rubbed his hands together and looked at Niva with glee in his eyes. "Curious?"

"Maybe we shouldn't get involved," Niva said cautiously.

"C'mon, let's see what it is," he said eagerly.

They made their way down to the beach as more people filled the narrow street. Pastor Cavanaugh stopped an elderly man. "What's happening?"

"The Messiah is here," he cried. "Here, and I must see him!"

Pastor Cavanaugh turned to Niva but she was now swept away from him by the ever-increasing crowds.

"Papa," Niva yelled, "Over here!"

Cavanaugh muscled his way towards her through the barrier of people, but the barrier moved like a surging human wave, pushing him towards the beach. He fell onto the warm sand, spotting a young girl rolling on the beach near a fishing boat. She tore at her clothes, spitting and screaming at those nearby. A tall slender man stood up from the boat and approached the girl.

Cavanaugh's heart beat hard. "Jesus! You are... Jesus!" he spluttered the words, feeling exhausted from the heave of people. "Niva's time calculations must be wrong."

When two fishermen of the twelve in the boat rose to their feet, Jesus raised his arm for them to sit down.

The girl on the beach writhed from side to side, clutching her abdomen. Her head shook violently, saliva pouring from her mouth as she kicked the sand. She scowled at Jesus. "Leave me be!"

"She has a demon!" cried one man.

The crowds gathered around the girl who could not have been more than ten years old. Her mother fought through the barrier of people and rushed to her side. She knelt before Jesus. "Her spirit is unclean, Lord."

Pastor Cavanaugh climbed onto a small boulder to examine the man from afar. "Looks like anyone else," he said, "not too tall, with eyes reflecting the morning sun like bonfires, and well-worn sandals about to break at the straps ... but what should he care for attire?"

His tangled hair and unshaped beard seem to glow from the light off the sea and Pastor Cavanaugh clasped his chest as he gaped at the man.

Jesus placed one hand on the girl's head. She fell limp on the sand, and a moment later she sat up quietly and smiled.

"Go now; I have made you well," Jesus said in warm tones.

Pastor Cavanaugh's gripped his chest. He looked at the stunned crowd and nodded slowly. "People are people, not too different emotionally from those of my time," he said quietly.

The girl stood up quickly and then ran to her mother's side.

One man pointed to the girl's mother and yelled, "She's a Canaanite woman, a worshipper of Baal!"

"But faith made the girl well," argued another.

"Go now," Jesus commanded. "And be at peace."

The crowds eventually dispersed in confusion and wonder. Jesus headed for the fishing boat.

Cavanaugh stumbled down from the boulder and followed him, his arms and legs trembling as he trudged through the sand.

Niva spotted her father from afar. "Papa—" she stopped herself.

Zane wondered if Niva had decided not to interrupt the moment the pastor had sought for so long.

Jesus bent over and unfolded his tunic to pick up some coins the locals had thrown to him. He stepped into the boat and dropped the coins for the fishermen to gather. All were laughing as Cavanaugh approached them.

"L-Lord," Cavanaugh stammered. "Jesus... Son of God—"

"Who calls? Healing time is over."

"What? Lord?" Pastor Cavanaugh shook nervously where he stood, ignoring the water lapping at his robes.

"You have a strange tongue," Jesus said. "Your Hebrew is unusual. Are you Roman?"

Pastor Cavanaugh staggered, his feet sinking into the sand. "This is the pinnacle of my spiritual life," he muttered under his breath.

"Well?" Jesus asked, stroking his beard with curiosity.

Cavanaugh gritted his teeth. "No," he said loudly. "Not Roman."

"Then do you speak Greek?"

"Yes."

"Fine. So what can I do for you?" Jesus instantly replied in fluent Greek.

"You healed a girl."

"Yes, by my Father's grace. But I must go now. There is much work to do."

"Lord," Cavanaugh insisted. "You must know who I am, do you not?"

"I do not."

"You are omni-everything," Cavanaugh said in English. "Do you understand me now?"

Jesus tilted his head. "Not familiar with this tongue," he said in Greek. "You look like a man of property. Perhaps you could give some shekels for the needy?"

A little girl ran past Pastor Cavanaugh, the same girl healed by Jesus only moments ago. "Our share!" she squealed, arms outstretched. "Our share, Jesus!"

Jesus placed two Roman copper coins in the palm of her hand. "Good fortune," he chuckled. "Eight quadrans for you."

Jesus eyed Cavanaugh suspiciously as the girl ran away. He raised a half-twisted smile and suddenly broke into raucous laughter.

Cavanaugh stumbled, his shoes sinking in the wet sand. Splashing in the incoming tide, he tried to steady himself.

The fishermen also rocked with laughter. Jesus knelt down in the boat to scoop a handful of coins, letting them trickle through his fingers. He stared coldly into the pastor's eyes. "One has to make a living."

Cavanaugh fell backwards into the wet sand. He gazed up into the heavy blue Mediterranean sky. His lips quivered. "What would they say back home?" He groaned and gripped his chest. He then tried to prop himself up on his elbows and felt an onset of dizziness as the light and laughter swelled around him. "I..." he forced his words while gasping for breath, "...should have studied law after all, for all it mattered in the world."

Jesus spoke aloud over the fishermen's convulsions of laughter, "Your words... they are strange." He glanced back at the fishermen who were counting their takings, and then offered a haughty flyaway grin, tossing his thick and tangled hair back with glee. "My performance must continue. The day has only just begun."

He climbed into the boat and muttered something Cavanaugh couldn't understand. One of the fishermen stood up and poled the boat into deeper water. The crew looked back at Cavanaugh, sniggering amidst indeterminate conversation.

With water lapping at his robes, Cavanaugh sat up slowly as the shock and disappointment tore across his face. Helpless, he watched the small boat and laughing crew set sail.

"Damn," he cursed, "Jesus Christ is a fraud."

11: On the Morrow

"Look at him, Zane, a broken man in the sand."

Zane whisked over to Angela's side, not seeming to care about the events that had just unfolded. "He probably had it coming."

"Maybe," she said quietly.

"Yeah," Zane said, "defeated by his own delusions. I didn't believe in him, not really."

"And now you're dead," Angela said flatly, "so as they say back in my home church – it's too late for the unbelieving dead to save themselves."

"You believed in Jesus? Most people believed. I was never sure anyway and I ain't seen him in the afterlife, only here... alive... pretty kooky, huh?"

"Ah!" Angela snapped her fingers.

Zane shrunk back in surprise. "What? Gee, those dead fingers of yours have a hall-effect sound... Anyway, I don't know how anyone could believe without proof."

"Depends on how you interpret what you see before you."

"What does that mean? Sounds funny coming from a ghost still lost in all of this. We've both seen the proof now," Zane said. "Look at him. The guys in the boat out there have shattered the poor pastor."

Angela spotted Niva racing across the sand. "Here she comes."

Niva threw herself to her father's side. "Papa! What on earth...?"

"The man's a fake," Cavanaugh cursed. "A con artist, a freak, a damn Greek actor!"

"Jesus?"

"Who else? He organizes mock miracles. He's probably some kind of magician too for all I know."

"Oh, Papa." Niva embraced his wet sand-smeared body, not caring about soiling her acquired clothes. "I wanted you to be finally happy and confirmed in true belief. Instead I've brought you down."

Her father broke into tears. "Nature," he blurted, "in its chaos has triumphed. There's nothing more to life."

"We have each other," Niva said softly. "We can love each other. There can still be love in the world, love and human dignity—"

"Ibi," someone yelled. "Vos!"

Two soldiers and a short bearded man ran towards them.

Niva shook her dazed father. "Papa, it must be the vineyard owner."

"Leave me here," he groaned.

Niva tugged at her father's clothes. "The guy we pinched these tunics from. Run!" She heaved his heavy frame without success.

Her father struggled to stand, unsteady in the wet sand.

"Desino! Vispilio!" The voices rang louder.

"C'mon, Papa; they're Romans. They might throw us to the lions."

"Nonsense," he groaned, dropping to the ground again. "Save yourself, child. I am done."

"No, you're not," Niva yelled, tugging at his arm. "I'm staying with you."

The two Romans confronted the pair. Niva opened her mouth to speak but was thrown to the sand. The vineyard owner ranted at them, flinging his arms in the air.

Pastor Cavanaugh blocked his ears.

"Silentium!" one of the soldiers barked. Both soldiers latched onto the pair and dragged them up the sand.

"I think that vineyard owner is pestering the soldier not to damage his clothes," Pastor Cavanaugh whispered to Niva.

The soldier cursed some unrecognizable words, waving his arms at the man and then pushed him away.

"They're in deep now," Zane said. "How do they get out of this one?"

"We could be stuck here," Angela said bluntly. "I think I see a funnel in the distance but it'd probably only take us somewhere else in this era."

"Wanna risk it?" Zane asked. "I'm a bit tired of witnessing grief and violence."

Angela's eyes narrowed as she glared at him. "I'm not leaving them," she said sternly. "Not for anything."

"Okay, okay. You're right of course, Ange." Zane said. "And what would I know?"

"Gotta stop running away from things, Zane." Angela said. "You did it when you were alive; now you do it when you're dead. I can see it in your eyes."

Zane swallowed hard and gazed back across the sea. He probed his mind to the time he had run away from home after an argument with Mom over Dad leaving them. He desperately wanted Dad to return and hoped he would if he knew his son had run away.

On a chilly night, Zane waited outside, hidden in the bushes, forever it seemed – he couldn't remember how long. He knew how crazy it was to wait in hiding for a guy who once called himself 'Dad'. And some time in the middle of the night amongst the cold swaying leaves and the newly-woven spider webs surrounding his damp seat of soil, Zane understood his father would never come back. Zane's heart panged with a hint of knowing that Dad probably never loved him, or Mom or Jen. And maybe he'd been running away from things ever since.

Zane swallowed again as he stared blankly at the sea. How could Angela know any of this? She's stinkin' guessing, he mused. She's a bit like me.

***

A small garrison fort lay to the south of Tyre. Zane and Angela hovered over a troop of Roman soldiers as they entered the gates. Pastor Cavanaugh and his daughter were hauled off the horses at the point of a sword and ordered to remove their tunics. When the guards saw what they wore underneath, they stepped back for a moment and eyed each other quizzically, then latched onto the pair, taking them to a dimly-lit cell.

Niva coughed. "Phew, it reeks."

"That's urine," Cavanaugh mumbled. "And excrement."

"Think I would prefer the Hollywood version to this," Niva huffed.

Zane and Angela melded through the thick stone walls, Zane dismissing the idea of floating through a couple of guards who stood blocking the doorway.

"Creeps me seeping through living people," Zane said.

"I've done it once and it felt creepy, but, other than that, people are just walking matter," Angela replied, "if you dismiss human aura fields, of course – but I know what you mean."

Zane gave a puzzled look. "But the soul within?"

"That doesn't take conscious form until death," she said. "Like a long gestation in life, life itself and the experience in life helps to shape the soul. Like a rebirth, I suppose; well, that's what the Dumpster Man says … after the body dies, but it doesn't work for everyone which sort of makes it confusing."

"Eh? Yeah, well, it's pretty creepy having human senses when we're dead," said Zane, looking around.

"I can actually smell the stinkin' shit in here – so gross."

"Never understood that either," Angela said. "We have nothing to smell, see and hear with and only our own representation of ourselves. Never figured how it worked. When I see that Dumpster Man again—"

A groan in the darkness caused her to turn.

Cavanaugh coughed and fell on a mat of straw. "Niva?"

"Yes, Papa, I'm here. I dare not sit in this light—"

Something groaned again.

Niva flung herself around.

Two eyes lit from a corner, glinting in the semi-light, as they slowly rose in the darkness.

Niva jumped back. "Who's there?"

A tattered old man emerged from the shadows, his face gaunt and angular. A hole appeared to be singed through his left cheek, probably from the push of a hot iron, Niva fearfully guessed. His bulging eyes glistened from the flame of a dying torch nearby.

"I have seen death too many times to count," the old man croaked.

Pastor Cavanaugh propped himself up against an uneven stone wall splashed in blotches of blackish red, he could only guess was old blood.

"Who are you?" he asked in Greek.

"A friend," the old man said feebly. "You wear strange clothes. Traders are you? Or robbers?"

"Robbers, unfortunately," Cavanaugh said.

"Robbers of the faith?"

Cavanaugh frowned at him and relayed the words to Niva in English. He eyed the old man carefully. "What do you mean... robbers of the faith?"

The old man toyed with his straggly, saliva-sodden beard, curling the wet gray strands around his finger. "These days, only those who believe in the Son of Man come to these cells. I am... was a wealthy Greek merchant. The Son of Man has shown me a better way. I reach for that faith like it is something so valuable and unattainable I just have to... steal it, even though it is essentially free."

Pastor Cavanaugh struggled to stand and Niva came to his side, lifting him with a groan.

Cavanaugh brushed the clinging moist straw from his clothes and eyed the man carefully, not sure whether to pity him or scold him. "The man you saw is a user, feeding off people's emotions and taking their money. Just try believing in yourself for a change. You may never have wound up in this place. Who wants a trickster for a leader?" He instantly thought of all the politicians in his time and then understood how difficult it can be to see the truth behind a face. He slapped the old man's bony shoulder and then gripped him hard with his both hands. "Have faith in... *yourself*."

Niva squeezed her father's arm and smiled warmly. She couldn't make out his words but felt his confidence returning.

"Idle words," the man grumbled. "I have seen his miracles. I believe—"

"Then I pity you." Cavanaugh turned his back on him and observed the small barred window above. He leant over to whisper in Niva's ear. "Tell me you brought it, that it's not in the time box and that you have it with you."

She tilted her head with a puzzled look.

"That laser contrivance. Tell me you have it."

A sudden grin lit her face. "Oh, yes, I always carry it." She dug deep into her pockets. "Somewhere on me," she said as she probed. "Ah!" She pulled out a button badge that read, *I love boys who love Jesus*. "Oh."

"That won't do us," her father said as he smiled.

The old man watched them with increasing perplexity as they spoke to each other in English.

Niva probed her back pockets. "Got it." She produced a transparent plastic mint container crammed with circuitry. "Cost me a bit to build and get it right," she said.

"Did it burn a hole in your pocket?" her father asked, half amused.

"Very funny," she said flatly.

The old man's eyes opened wider as Niva switched on the beam and aimed it at the bars, the laser slicing through slowly. The light flickered for a moment but continued.

"Power source fades quickly using several watts of power. At least these bars are corroded."

"Who..." the old man wailed, "who are you?"

"Just people like you," Pastor Cavanaugh said firmly.

Niva gripped the sliced bars and shrunk back. "Ouch! Still a bit hot."

Her father took out a handkerchief and helped her push out the old bars. They creaked and separated easily from the stone which crumbled away.

"Look, this cell is partly below ground, like the cellar back home," Niva said. "I can just reach the soil outside. Help me up, Papa."

Pastor Cavanaugh lifted his daughter to the window and she wriggled her body through the narrow opening, ripping one of her pockets on a jagged piece of iron.

"Your turn, Papa."

Her father scratched his head. "I'm somewhat rotund. Think I'll get through?"

"You have to." She reached out to him. "C'mon."

Pastor Cavanaugh turned to the old man and spoke in Greek. "Coming?"

The old man stepped back with an uncertain gaze.

"Help me up," he said as best he could in Greek, "then I'll reach and grab your arms." He held out both open hands and gave a pushing motion with his arms.

The old man hesitated and then stepped forward and heaved the pastor through the opening as he gasped for air.

Pastor Cavanaugh took a deep breath, pulling his stomach in as far as he could.

Outside, Niva pulled her father through the opening and, when he was through, he turned and reached in for the old man whose arms wavered as they probed into the daylight.

Pastor Cavanaugh gripped soiled and aged hands, wondering if the bones would slip out from the leathery palms that contained them. He heaved the man upwards. "You're heavy for someone so frail," he panted.

Something clanged from the darkness inside.

The old man suddenly jerked backwards, pulling Pastor Cavanaugh's head against the wall. Someone flung a sword out through opening, striking Cavanaugh's arm and slicing through fabric and skin.

"Papa!" Niva shrieked.

The rocky face of a Roman guard lunged out of the darkness, the point of his sword just missing Pastor Cavanaugh's eye. Niva tugged at her father, pulling him away just in time.

"Horses," Niva said and pointed.

Pastor Cavanaugh nursed his arm as they dashed clumsily for the horses tied up nearby.

Niva helped her father into the saddle. "Hope this Arab is a fast one," she said quickly. "Hang on..."

She sat behind her father and gripped the reins, struggling with the horse and finally managing to get the mare going.

"Bet you wished you went on that horse-riding camp now," her father said. He looked behind as a guard struggled through the cell window, yelling back at the other guards. More guards appeared from another entrance nearby.

"They'll be onto us in a flash. Faster, Niva!"

Niva dug her heels in and they galloped through the small town, causing a stir as they passed more women with pads and water jars, one of the jars falling and shattering on the stony path that wound out of town.

Her father groaned.

"That arm needs looking at," Niva said.

"Faster," he gasped. He spotted the loculus in the hazy distance. "Look, the cube..."

Niva glanced behind her and spotted a large cloud of dust in the air over the rise. "There's a whole Roman troop behind us!"

She finally eased back the reins as they arrived at the loculus and slid off to help her father down. "How's that arm?"

"It'll keep. Let's just get inside this thing."

Niva thumbed the garage door opener. "Won't open; it won't work," she squealed, "Why now?"

Zane asked, "How do they get out of this one? We could be stuck here in this stinkin' place with them."

"Do you always think of yourself?"

Zane shrugged and knew Angela was right.

"Give it to me," Pastor Cavanaugh said urgently.

She bit her lip and handed him the control and he removed the square battery, pressing the connection terminals against his tongue. "Has a charge; must be a poor connection."

Niva looked back at the building cloud of dust. She could now hear the thumping hoofs and clanging armor. "Give me the control, Papa."

"Hold on," he said firmly as he snapped the battery lit shut. "Here, try it now."

Niva took it quickly and aimed the control at the loculus. The door instantly materialized and hissed open.

"Not bad, Papa, not bad at all."

They jumped through the entrance and the door hissed to a close behind them, reintegrating with the loculus wall just as the troop arrived in a swirl of desert dust.

Niva flicked a few switches. "Oh no," she whined, "the charge isn't complete..."

The walls bowed from the push of the soldiers outside. An instrument panel sparked, a hazy white smoke filling the loculus.

Pastor Cavanaugh pressed himself against the weakest part of the loculus where the door normally appeared. "Can't hold on much longer," he said breathlessly. "Losing strength ... have we any energy at all, just to scare them away?"

"No," Niva said, her eyes beginning to stream. "It's hopeless. I could deflect energy into the walls to make the material substructure stronger but we would never leave this place. It'd be a matter of time before they broke through. As the energy weakens, so do the walls." She tore at her hair. "What do I do?"

"Just hit any button," her father yelled. "Something'll work; it's got to."

"Is that faith?"

The loculus swayed and began to tilt, the inner walls creaking. The banging against the loculus walls resonated so loudly Niva wondered what they were using to try to get in. She slipped on the floor grid, sliding to the opposite control bank as the loculus tilted further.

"They must have the whole garrison out there. They're trying to tip us over!"

The loculus dropped back, throwing her father to the floor.

Zane whizzed around the confines of the loculus. "Okay, so how do they get out of this one?"

Angela glanced sideways and floated back towards the central column. "I don't like this feeling I'm getting."

171

Zane scrunched his face. "What?"

And then the rocking of the loculus was suddenly subdued; it sat in silence.

Pastor Cavanaugh struggled up and reached for the camera control. He flicked the monitor switch but only swirling dust showed on the small screen. He shuddered and glanced sideways. An orange mist grew from the corner behind him, filling the small room.

He swung about quickly to catch a glimpse of his daughter disappearing in the mist. "Niva?"

A figure moved from behind the central column. A face emerged from the mist, the face of a man with wiry, balding hair and no beard. He approached Pastor Cavanaugh and smiled slightly.

Niva's father stood aghast before the stranger.

"Papa?"

Niva probed her way along the edge of the control panel to her father's side.

Pastor Cavanaugh gulped and opened his mouth to speak but Niva stepped in front of him, hands on hips. "How'd you get in here?

"Niva, he won't understand you. Let me—"

"You wish to see me," the stranger said in English.

Pastor Cavanaugh stood back aghast. The man's eyes never left his. He seemed to speak from those eyes, a bright azure.

"Are you... Are you...?"

"The one you seek," The stranger said. He raised his arms. His wrists bore two blood-stained holes. "This is what you want to see?"

Pastor Cavanaugh fell back against the instrument panel, his jaw opening.

Angela gaped at the man and then quickly melded into the central column and peered back through the density, and whispered, "You!"

Zane hovered behind the column and probed with his arm to touch Angela. "You okay?"

Angela didn't answer.

Niva also gaped at the man, who was slender and wore a white tunic that draped down to tattered sandals. "You're not Jesus," she said softly under her breath. She nodded her head slowly. "Yes, another time traveler. Nobody else could have breached this loculus." And then she noticed the holes in his hands and stepped back. She tried to force the words. "You... you are the Christ?"

"You say I am. I am. But I know what you are thinking."

Niva gulped.

"I span the centuries," Jesus said.

"But my calculations, this time, right now," Niva said. "You should be... you should be in Jerusalem."

Pastor Cavanaugh waved his hand at her. "Now, child, all the calculations of humankind couldn't have brought a better moment than this."

"You were late by several days," Jesus said softly. "I have been on wood and now return to my Father."

Niva tore her eyes away from the man's captivating, blue-eyed stare. She flicked a few controls on the panel and concentrated on the digital time settings. "Dates," she mumbled, "Calendars... Julian, Gregorian..."

Pastor Cavanaugh placed his hand softly on her shoulder. "I know now. We are out by eleven or so days, my child. A handful of days wiped clean by Pope Gregory. Our humble human efforts have overlooked the obvious. That's our fallibility."

He dropped to his knees at the feet of their visitor. "Lord, forgive me."

"Stand up!" Jesus said firmly.

Another face emerged momentarily from the misted shadows, a more familiar face bearing a soft, glowing smile.

"Mama!" Niva cried.

"Susan!" Pastor Cavanaugh held out his arms.

Both lunged for the shadows but the face had already dispersed into the swirls of mist and she could hear what sounded like hundreds of voices mumbling, whispering and almost chanting in the distance before they too faded.

She punched her way furiously through the mist, waving it aside in futility.

"Mama, wait!"

Pastor Cavanaugh stood frozen, arms outstretched towards the vanishing light that was his wife.

Jesus looked at him and nodded. "In time," he said softly.

And then Jesus glanced at Zane.

Zane felt a surge run through every glowing corner of his being, pulsating behind his eyes in painful jabs. He slipped backwards to meld into a bank of switches.

Pastor Cavanaugh slowly dropped his arms, his face streaming. "Lord, I always wanted to know. Why did you visit this time, the time of the Jews during Roman occupation? Why did you not come to our most troubled age first?"

"If I wait and go to your age first, there would be nothing to go to. For without the light of my spirit from this time forth, there would be no world to visit in your time. You will have all burned yourselves long ago." He turned to the same vertical slit of light Susan

Cavanaugh had slipped into. "I am summoned. My destination now is what you would call another world around another sun."

Pastor Cavanaugh stood in awe as the surrounding vapors abated through the channel of light closing behind Jesus. At that moment a rising hum of power brought all instrumentation alive. Niva clutched her father's arm and her father noticed it too. The wound made by the guard had healed completely. He looked up at Jesus, but he was gone.

"I wonder what happened to the Romans outside?" she asked. She flicked a few switches and viewed the monitor connected to the external camera pod. She slowly turned the joystick control as both stared at the scene. In the settling dust they could see the soldiers on the ground, most face-down in the sand. Niva turned up the volume and could hear some soldiers crying, while others moaned and gripped their heads. Swords and shields were scattered some distance beyond, glinting in the sunlight. "What's with their weapons? Did some … *power* fling them out of their hands?" She panned the camera upwards and could see in the distant dust haze the horses galloping away –riderless.

"My God," her father said slowly. He fell back on the chair and shook his head while biting his lower lip.

He took in a deep breath. "We should return home. Though I don't know what we'd be heading back to."

"People will need us," Niva said quietly, "more than ever." She tapped the old brass gauges. "Strap in, Papa."

Pastor Cavanaugh dropped his head in his hands and mumbled through his fingers. "So many questions." His words filled the silence as they both looked at each other and contemplated their visitor. "I am so dumb-struck by the reality of it all," he said.

Niva looked at her father with a mix of shock, awe and love. "I wonder if we'll ever see Mama again."

"Did this really happen? Did we really see Jesus?" Pastor Cavanaugh asked.

A distant voice came from the corner where Jesus had departed. Both father and daughter heard it distinctly.

"*Go back to your age. I shall see you on the morrow.*"

"He saw me, Ange. He was looking right at me," Zane said uneasily.

"Not the pastor again," she said dismissively.

"No, Jesus!"

"I..." She paused, tapping her lip. "Just can't be, looks a bit different—"

Zane broke into nervous laughter. "Looks a bit like that balding singer dude on television doing a comeback tour. What's his name?"

"Dork, Zane. You're a dork. That's not what I mean. I mean, he's…"

"What? What's with you?" He floated to Angela's side, a look of concern filling his eyes while, behind them, Niva took control of the loculus and jerked the time cube into motion.

"He wasn't always bald," Angela said.

"So? Jake's dad wasn't always bald. What about… whoa!" Zane felt his spirit pulling itself apart as the loculus jolted.

"Hang onto something, Ange."

"We're too far from the central column, it's hard to hold on to anything," she cried. "I feel weak all of a sudden."

"Me too… The walls…" Zane pointed a shaky finger at the walls of the loculus which now glowed. "Must be an effect of returning to where we came from, but Niva and her father don't seem to notice anything odd about the cube."

"It's pulling us through the walls!" Angela screeched. "We'll be lost forever!"

Their two spirits sifted through the loculus wall to the outside.

Zane saw a rainbow trail of light snaking away from the time cube into infinity in a hazy indigo void. He flung his arm out to grab her, the other latching and melding with what felt like part of the grid at the base of the cube which didn't rotate.

"Angela, please try to hang onto me," he cried. He watched his arm stretch eerily, thinking it was like stretching chewing gum.

"Can't hold much longer," she screamed.

Zane's arm began to dissolve and he felt it begin to slowly tear away like cotton wool. He glanced ahead, looking down, as the time cube arced towards a shape in the distance. "There's a kind of round exit and stars on the other end. We're heading for it. Just a bit further, Ange."

An immense blackness then swallowed the loculus, accompanied by a crackling sound. Zane and Angela shot through the air into the twilight of a new landscape.

"Cutting it close," Zane breathed.

"Bad choice of words, but we're in one piece," she said, forcing a smile. "And look, there's the old church... or what's left of it."

"But that loculus thing has left us behind; I don't see it, Ange."

"Where could it have gone?"

179

"Beats me… a bit further into the future?"

Zane swept closer to the ground. Pieces of shattered stained glass glistened in the moonlight. He hovered towards an undulated graveyard, the stones pushed up over the years by the movement of soil and tree roots. He remembered when he saw graveyards like this as a child and used to think they were the dead trying to push their way out of the ground without success. Zane suddenly felt tired and hadn't really thought about sleep until now. He wondered if ghosts actually sleep, and then he wondered about Jesus.

"Hey, Ange, that Jesus guy."

"What?"

"If he's Jesus, why are we still in this in-between state? Heaven must exist, after all."

"And Hell as well," she said bluntly, rolling her eyes.

"Doesn't he know us? Doesn't he know everything?"

"He certainly knows me," she said flatly.

"What do you mean by that?"

She stared blankly at the grave stones. A shell had blown apart an old mound; the headstone lay shattered across the path before them.

"Well?" Zane prompted, "You've been flying around this crazy afterlife longer than I have. And the only other spirit I have seen is you. Why? Where has every other dead dude gone to? They can't all be stuck in their own Hells, surely."

"I've seen other spirits," she said, her face turning glum. "I told you before I had a friend ghost who was taken."

"Yeah? Where?"

"Stop moving, Zane. You look like a funny glowing bouncing bubble. Assume your form. I need to see you."

Zane had forgotten his relaxed state had caused his shape to become amorphous. For the first time he felt safe, away from people – not that they could really hurt him. More importantly, he was away from events that shocked and freaked him. "So where are these spirits?"

Angela looked away. "They're lonely spirits. They don't like to leave their death zones, the places where their bodies died. They hang around in the real world."

"Like ghosts haunting old castles?" Zane chuckled.

"It's not funny," she snapped.

"Hey, what's up?"

"Back then," she started, "back before I met you, I came across a spirit named Ed. Dead Ed I called him—"

"Dead head," Zane said under his breath and chuckled.

"Stop it. Anyway, he was older and hadn't run into other older ghosts, only young ghosts like us. He had made a lot on the stock market and had a big house and had worked hard for it and didn't want to leave the place. He was lonely when alive, all his family long gone, but loneliness didn't seem to bother him."

"So what happened?"

"I had to go. I just had to leave," she said, the sparkle of a tear emerging from her eye.

Zane felt confused and didn't know whether to hold her with a tingling hug or look away with embarrassment. He looked up to a night sky that was mostly clear, except for some clouds in the distance. Some of the stars above appeared to be slowly moving. He drew beside her, his aura tingling against hers. "Sorry Ange. Did Dead Ed hurt you?"

"No," she said quietly. "He died."

"Huh? Died? But he was already dead!"

"Died again, died completely, Zane – ceased to exist altogether; I'm sure of it."

"What? But how?"

"I told you before but you wouldn't listen..." Angela said as she looked up at the sky. Her eyes opened wide, her face glowing brighter with instant fear, and she spoke more hurriedly, "He was taken the same way we'll be, if we don't move right now!"

"What?"

She gripped Zane's glowing hand, tugging him away from the ground. "Look up!" she ordered, pointing to the sky.

Zane looked up again. "Hey, those stars are really moving." The moving stars he saw earlier were larger, and swirling and spiraling down towards them.

"They're not stars – or satellites," Angela said hurriedly. "They're Munchers! That's what I tried to tell you earlier, what the Dumpster Man called them. They got Dead Ed and would have got me. We must find a funnel fast!"

Zane watched the lights not only appear larger as they neared, their size seemed to expand more rapidly also. They pulsated from a yellow glow within and a sound like a high-pitched dental drill shrilled across the valley.

"Zane, a funnel – over there," she said quickly. "Hang onto my hand."

Angela swooped low over the trees with Zane barely keeping up, the orbs of light closing in.

"They're like homing ghosts!" Zane shrieked. "How'd they find us?"

"It's our energy, he says," Angela yelled. "They want our particulate energy."

Zane didn't have time to mull over what she had just said. They reached a small funnel, brightly lit in the sky. Zane could feel the spirit cloud slowly fold over them, the familiar force of wind propelling them into the funnel entrance.

"Oh, Zane, look out!"

Something burned through his shoe. He swung back to see but had to cover his eyes. A wide circle of throbbing light had latched onto his foot, the throbbing intensifying around the tip of his shoe. Zane felt it seep through to bite his toes with intense cold but it felt intensely hot at the same time. He jerked his leg back, but the orb of light persisted as if glued to him. He began to feel weak, his eyes blinded by the orb and what appeared to be two dark bluish circles within, like a pair of menacing dark eyes, perhaps. Zane forced his eyes open just a fraction. Those two darker circles narrowed like closing eyes, the darkness within turning black.

"Zane!" Angela tugged at his fading spirit, the light of his being dimming before her.

"C-can't," he stammered, "budge... feel sleepy."

184

Angela wrenched with all her strength at Zane's now shapeless form.

The funnel entrance around them closed quickly inwards and Zane felt the biting light relax its hold on him and finally release to fall away as the funnel walls expelled the throbbing orb back out into the night behind them.

Zane fell back against the spongy funnel walls and looked at Angela solemnly as he nursed his foot. "I felt pain, real pain. Now I'm really scared. There were eyes in there. Those things have eyes."

"We got away, Zane."

"Thanks to you. You're stronger than you look, Ange."

"I couldn't save Ed," she said sadly. "He didn't want to fight them, like he lost his will or something. I had to leave him." Her eyes were near black now, the edges glistening blue from the swell of tears.

"It's okay," Zane said softly. "You saved me, didn't ya?"

Angela looked up at the bright walls of the funnel. She wiped a tear from a face more pallid than her ghostly usual. "Maybe this funnel was too light for the Muncher to penetrate."

"But they're light too. What's the difference?"

"Beats me," she said. "Just guessing, but I heard they can't get through every funnel, only some. Maybe this one was narrower than the edge of the Muncher light, though it's hard to tell, the way these funnels swell and contract. We're lucky, Zane." She looked down. "And I didn't help you more than this funnel did."

"Don't worry about it," Zane insisted. "And as for Dead Ed, how can you blame yourself?"

Angela smiled slightly and her eyes returned more to the deep blue-green haze that seemed normal for her appearance in this afterlife.

Zane glanced back at the narrowing funnel mouth they had entered. The Muncher lights wheeled around the entrance but didn't follow them in.

"Like a safety valve to another world, this funnel," he said.

"The Munchers never got close enough to touch me," she said. "I remember the Dumpster Man talking about their eyes. He said they're like black pearl eyes without a body, floating in light."

"That burning," Zane said slowly. "Where do these things come from? Are they made from the same energy as us?"

"Lord knows," Angela said.

186

Zane stared at her blankly. "Speaking of lord, what ever happened to that dude we saw in the time box – you know, Jesus? He could have got us out of this pickle for sure."

She shook her head. "Zane, I must tell you something about that Jesus."

Zane was looking down the funnel as they progressed, picturing himself riding a jet through a cloud haze, or perhaps a magic carpet. "Hey, there's an exit already."

Angela spotted the exit and shook her head. "Not again."

"What? What's wrong?" Zane squinted to see. A gray mass grew larger as they approached the exit. "That's not cloud. It's too smooth. Looks like a wall. This funnel is throwing us at a wall!"

"Unnerving, this kind of exit," Angela said. "Last time I exited a funnel like this, I wound up several hundred feet below ground. Thought I saw dinosaur bones and a big cave but I was in such a panic to get out into the air. It's very disorientating. At least we're not going too fast in this funnel." She gripped Zane's hand. "But hang on."

In a gush of spirit wind, they exited the funnel to find themselves pressed against the gray surface. It was a bitumen surface. Zane tilted his head sideways and mumbled through pressed lips. "I see grass in the distance. Why do I feel squashed?"

"Melding exit," Angela said. "Sometimes we meld with the matter we encounter, like we sort of did in Mister Numan's house."

"And like I did in the time machine? Hey, I hope they're okay back there."

"Yes, they'll be fine," Angela said, wondering why she just said that and how she could possibly know.

"Push away from the surface, Zane."

Zane pressed himself hard against the bitumen. "Feels like Velcro! Cool!" He sprang back and swung to look around, staring at the skewed horizon. The landscape slowly rotated and he gained his bearings. He looked at Angela and she looked back, smiling.

Zane broke into a laugh. "Hey, we're in a schoolyard."

"So far, so good," she said, "Nothing weird about that."

Zane noticed a familiar basketball hoop, the backboard covered in graffiti. "Hey, we're in my schoolyard!"

"Zane," Angela said. "About Jesus. He looked different, but—"

"Yeah... not much hair. And I don't care what you say, the guy saw me, too."

"*...He who aspires...*"

"No!" Zane clutched his head and fell back slowly, staring blankly into space. Angela had seen that expression on his face before and knew the hidden voice had returned.

Zane turned slowly to her. "You can't hear this, can you, right?"

Blank-faced, Angela shook her head and shrugged.

"Why?" Zane screamed to the sky, gripping his head as the words beat through his ears,

"He who aspires comes to naught,
When oppressed by those around,
Yet when he stokes a daydream thought,
Fruits of reality will astound."

The words faded quickly and Zane sat up again, still holding his ears. "Doesn't work. Nothing works! Why do I get this voice in my head?"

Angela sat and looked impatient. "Zane, I don't know what's going on with you and the voice but I simply have to tell you about the Jesus we saw in the loculus."

Zane moaned from the grating words in his ears until something caught his eye and he sat up quickly and pointed. "Look!"

Angela looked towards the swings. Someone lay slumped on the ground – a boy around Zane's age.

Zane's heart pounded as he squinted to see; the thumping seemed to push back the voice in his head. He stared hard at the boy whose face was covered in blood.

"I recognize him, Zane," Angela said with distress. "He was at your funeral."

"Gotta go," Zane said, getting up.

"What can you do?" Angela frowned. "I must tell you about Jesus. I know now who he is!"

"Yeah, he's Jesus!" Zane shouted as he left her side. He dashed over to the swings to examine Alfred who lay on the bitumen in a semi-conscious daze.

Angela fell back on the ground and mumbled to herself, "Jesus is the Dumpster Man."

12: Children of the Midnight

"Alfred!" Zane cried. He circled around his friend who lay motionless on the bitumen. A gash of blood oozed through Alfred's curly red hair.

"Alfred!" he yelled again. *As if he's going to respond.*

Zane clutched his face with anxiety. His fingers sank into his vaporous cheeks. There was nothing he could do. His fingers slipped further into his cheeks and he flung them out again with a kind of dread that was always with him. He gazed around the schoolyard. Some children played in the distance but no one seemed to notice Alfred Wilson sprawled on the bitumen.

"Zane?" Alfred whispered. "That you?'

Zane swung about and stared at him in disbelief.

Alfred's lips barely moved. "Zane?"

"I'm here," Zane gasped. "I don't know how you can hear me, but I'm here with you."

"Zane," Alfred repeated.

"Over there!" cried a voice behind them.

Zane spotted a teacher, Mister Callister, and a pupil he didn't know rushing towards them. Mister Callister knelt down and examined the wounds on Alfred's forehead. "Wilson, can you hear me? Who did this?"

Alfred's eyelids opened slightly, his eyes glazed in the cold afternoon sun. He shivered and probed the air with an uncertain hand as the cold air pressed against his injury, causing it to throb. "Zane," he said weakly and swayed his head. "Zane..."

Mister Callister looked at the other pupil with confusion. "Does he mean Zane Carter?"

"Zane's dead," the other pupil said.

"He's confused from the bump," Mister Callister replied.

"Zane was Alfred's friend," the pupil continued.

"Ah." Mister Callister nodded. "Alfred. Who did this to you?"

"I'm here, Alfred, I'm here," Zane said urgently.

"I can see you," Alfred said deliriously. I..." His eyes closed again and he passed out.

Mister Callister whipped out his cell phone and nailed the keypad with hurried fingers.

"You'll be alright," Zane said to Alfred reassuringly. "Though I'm stumped how you could hear me, I know you'll be okay. You're not ready to die, buddy. I feel it. Hang on, pal."

Zane flew out of the way of Mister Callister, who waved at another approaching teacher.

Zane eyed the other pupil whom he didn't know and wondered how the kid knew anything about him. People talk, he mused. Not that I did anything much to be remembered by.

"Say, Angela, did people at school talk about you after you died?" Zane looked about, expecting her to hover over to him with a reply.

Angela was gone.

A faint wailing sound began to fill the air and Zane knew the ambulance was approaching. He overheard the unknown pupil talking about Matt. Zane guessed it was Matt Higgins and probably his pals who beat up Alfred.

"Higgins, so you did this to Alfred... asshole." Zane swept his eyes across the schoolyard. Angela was nowhere to be seen and he wondered if another funnel had taken her away or if she was exploring the school or just hiding nearby for some ridiculous reason.

Two paramedics approached with a stretcher and Zane spotted the hospital name on the ambulance nearby. He hovered over Alfred, still wondering how a beaten-up boy could hear a dead guy speak. "I'll catch up with you, buddy. Right now I gotta find someone, but I'll be back to see if you're okay." He zoomed up from the schoolyard and scanned the school buildings. Angela was nowhere to be seen. Zane swung down towards the buildings at the far end of the school. Higgins will be down there in Geography, he thought, unless he's back of the gym smoking again. He wondered why Angela was not around and tried to put such unsettling thoughts aside while he pondered a kind of revenge for Alfred. But this is dumb, he thought. What can I do?

Zane glanced through the window into the geography class. Higgins was at the back of the class, tilting back his chair to rest precariously against the wall behind. He sat, seemingly fatter than before with a mauled pencil in his mouth. Zane could hear the occasional crunch of teeth on wood as Higgins casually mulled over a graffiti-covered textbook on his lap.

Zane then spotted Jake on the other side of the class, flicking his pen like a fan. He obviously appeared bored and Zane nodded with agreement. Mister Ainsworth circled his laser pointer over a computer-projected map on the whiteboard. It looked like a troop movement map with icons of tanks and soldiers littered across it. All he talks about is war, Zane thought. He should have been a history teacher.

Something crashed at the back of the class. Everyone turned about to see that Higgins had fallen off his chair again.

"Higgins, how many times do I have to tell you not to lean on your chair?"

Zane breathed an uneasy smile but felt comforted that not much had changed in his school, that life goes on and people get on with living while he has to get on with being dead. And now he had to find out what happened to Alfred and Angela for that matter.

"Sorry, Sir," Higgins groaned, as he struggled to stand and right his chair. Jake spat with laughter after trying to hold back a chuckle. He spoke under breath, "Total dumb wit."

"I heard that," Higgins snarled.

"Okay, that'll do," Mister Ainsworth continued. "Now about the peak oil fields—"

With a hard knuckle-rap on the door, Mister Callister entered and whispered in Ainsworth's ear, and then he waited in the corridor outside.

Mister Ainsworth eyed Higgins and put his pen in his pocket. He approached him silently as the rest of the class turned their gaze to follow their teacher.

"Matthew Higgins, you are wanted in the Principal's office right now."

"Me?" Higgins asked defiantly.

"Right now, Higgins."

"—Sir," Higgins got up quickly, the back of his legs flicking the chair behind him into the wall.

"Yes!" Jake breathed, clenching his fist.

Ainsworth glanced at Jake. "Enough of that, Numan." He placed his hand on Higgins's shoulder and motioned him out of the room. "On your way, lad … again."

Higgins strolled past Jake, his shirt tail hanging out. He glared at Jake and slobbered his words as the pencil never left his mouth. "You're on my list, Numan."

Zane followed them out of the building, gliding along the path leading to the Principal's office. He scanned the grounds for Angela but couldn't see her. A number of funnels swayed in the air some distance away. She could have gone through any of them. She could be gone for good.

***

Angela swooped low over the corn fields that stretched to the horizon. She thought this could be anywhere but it did seem familiar, not too many miles from her father's factory perhaps. She wondered if the factory was still cordoned off, or running at all, and she wasn't sure if she really wanted to know.

The moon was low and lit the fields in a haze of soft silvery gold tips that swayed in the evening breeze. She wondered how such a funnel could scoop her away from Zane's schoolyard and perhaps take her back so close to home and she could only presume the Dumpster Man had directed her here somehow. She passed over an old junkyard where not a single hint of light reflected from the twisted and torn wreckage, jutting out their awkward shapes into the night sky. She wondered if he was down there, waiting, but she also knew he visited many junkyards.

A few miles she thought. If only I can get my bearings, I could find home and see if Mom's okay. It's been so long.

She flew over a forested area and spotted small lights blinking through the trees. "A village or town?" she asked herself. It would be a good starting place to get my bearings, she thought. She darted her glowing shapeless form through the trees and flew into a glade surrounded by old buildings with stretched verandahs and wicker chairs which creaked in the strong evening breeze. The streets were empty and the only light came from the old-fashioned street lamps mounted on ornate cast iron posts. She wondered if it was late. Oh, for a watch, she mused, but then time always seemed to shift a little from place to place as she traveled the funnels.

"Another," someone whispered nearby.

"Another," someone else repeated.

Angela spun about, looking into every dark corner of the small town, but she could see nothing. A light came on from a weatherboard cottage nearby and somebody opened the door. "Curse ye," said an old man in a savage voice and waved a broom. "Be gone! Don' bother us tonight. The Devil take ye!"

Angela stared hard at the old man. A small light hovered before him, and then flew in circles around his head. The old man dropped the broom and cupped his ears and stumbled back inside, slamming the door.

Angela felt her heart thumping madly as she gasped to herself, "Another ghost!"

The small light instantly halted and took the form of a little girl. Angela could hear her giggling in the empty night.

"Another," a voice said, this time closer.

Angela realized this was not such an empty place after all. The little girl spotted her and floated towards her. More ghosts seeped out from the houses nearby, from the trees, lamp posts, a mail box and a newspaper stand. One of the older ghosts appeared to struggle as he pushed his flickering form through a brick wall. Angela became surrounded by the glowing eyes of more than twenty children, constantly circling her or swirling up and down before her.

"Another, we found another!" cried a small boy ghost. He could not have been more than six years old.

"Soon we'll have an army!" exclaimed a taller, older boy, perhaps eleven or twelve, Angela thought. He approached her, his arm outstretched and he spoke with confidence, "Welcome to Ghost Brigade One, Midnight Division. I'm Captain Carlos. And this is Peter, little Vanessa, Michael, Stephanie, Neil and the rest of the brigade." He dropped his arm. "And you are?"

"Angela Moore," she replied slowly. She felt a little stunned by all the sudden life of a sort, displaying their energies before her. "Where are you all from? Here?"

"Oh no," said the little girl Angela first saw. "We come from—"

"Shhhhh," hissed another kid ghost. "Can we trust her?"

"She's like us," Carlos said with a shrug. "She's not a baddy like *them*," he said confidently. "I can tell."

Angela relaxed a little at that remark and hovered to rest on the mail box. "So if you're not all from here, where are you from?"

"Mexico," Carlos said proudly.

"Kansas," said Neil.

"Sydney," said Vanessa, the little girl ghost.

"Wow," said Peter, eyes wide. "You came a long way."

"And how come you're all here?" Angela asked.

"I dunno," said Vanessa, the coy little girl who suddenly grinned mischievously.

"This is a suitable place for training," Carlos said. "We will train and the General will be happy."

"The General?"

"General Jack Napes, our teacher," Carlos said, a little surprised. "Didn't Spook School send you?"

"I... err..."

"Ah," Carlos nodded. "Then you have not yet been called. General Jack is also known as The Gatherer. His followers round up young ghosts like you to teach them the tricks to be a really good ghost."

"Or bad," said Peter, while pretending to swing off a tree branch.

"Enough!" Carlos snapped. "We are here to teach the living a lesson, to stop them from being complacent."

"By spooking them?" Angela asked. "By making things go bump in the night? How can you make them see you or the things you do? How do you make things go bump?"

"There are ways," Carlos said confidently. "You will learn them too."

"How long have you been here?"

"A while."

Angela suddenly gripped her face with fear. "Munchers, how do you keep clear of them?

"Munchers?" Carlos asked. "Oh yes, they don't bother us. General Napes makes sure of that."

Angela wondered who this Napes guy was. The only ghost she had met with any kind of wisdom was the Dumpster Man and not even he had offered her any advice on keeping the Munchers away. Maybe 'Gatherer' was another word for 'Reaper' and that thought sent a ripple through her. "How does Napes do it? Keep the Munchers away?"

Carlos gave Angela an intensely curious stare. "Just how did you find us?"

"I don't quite know," she said. "I thought perhaps the Dumpster Man led me here."

"Dumpster Man?" Carlos shrieked, *"Him?"* He suddenly morphed his form into a glowing ball and bounced himself around the sidewalk, laughing incessantly.

"What?" Angela fumed.

"Dumpster Man? No way! He's an old coot with as much sense of the afterlife as a frog crossing the road about to meet it."

"How would you know?" Angela asked defiantly.

"Because the General says so. He says that trash man has no purpose and will go on through death until he sort of rots."

"Impossible," Angela said.

"As in dissolves into nothing, so not even a Muncher would be satisfied," Carlos said with a sick laugh.

"I'm getting bored," said another ghost. "Let's bother Mister Perkins."

"No," Carlos said decisively. "His quota of scares is full today. We don't want to completely scare people away. That's not our purpose. We don't want to turn this place into a ghost town."

"A town for ghosts," Peter laughed from the tree. "Hey, that's us."

Peter appeared to be older than Carlos, and Angela wondered why he didn't assume leadership of this ghostly rabble.

"I want to go home," sobbed a tiny voice in the background.

"Too late for that," Carlos said.

The wind suddenly picked up to a howling gale and Angela spotted the air itself appear to shred apart with luminous vapors feathering and streaking away with the wind.

"The Gatherer is returning," Carlos said.

Angela didn't like the feel of this place, these ghosts who seemed to be aimless though controlled by some kind of faculty. As well, the opening light that tore through the atmosphere unsettled her.

The wisps of light changed colors; like a rainbow they traversed the ever widening holes tearing into this world to dance freely in the new air. The colors reminded her of something she had seen elsewhere but she couldn't quite grasp the memory right now as a sudden fear began to ripple through her increasingly jittery fingers.

She rose up quickly from the mailbox and dashed down the street, spotting a sign that read: *You are leaving Spoonville, please come back soon.*

Sure, she thought cynically, Spooksville more like it. The name rang a bell with her and she remembered a village not far from Coopersville, near her father's factory. It was supposed to be a ghost town until redeveloped by the city council.

She noticed half of the houses were unlit in the night and appeared to be vacant, so no doubt new residents were being spooked away.

She quickly glanced over her shoulder. The other ghosts hadn't appeared to notice her departure. They hovered carefully above the opening rift of rainbow vapors and swirling winds which swayed the branches of the surrounding trees. "What could be powerful enough to do that?" she asked herself. But she didn't want to hang around to find out – she just wanted to get out of here quickly.

She propelled her now shapeless form down the street, glancing every so often to see what was happening behind her. The emerging light was now complete, every colored thread in the air now joined to make the loose and shifting circle surrounding an old oak door which materialized before the children. But, instead of opening, it dissolved to reveal a passageway filtering into the air. She spotted the silhouette of a man stepping through the opening but she was too far away to make out his features. She stared intently but could only make out he was wearing some kind of military uniform. Whoever it was, she didn't feel quite ready to face him and be taken to a weird school. She hated school while alive. She turned and sped through the forest from where she came, sifting her form through the soft leaves of trees that didn't seem to care for the commotion back there in that little town. Poor locals, she thought.

She flew for miles over the corn fields in the quiet and empty night. She finally spotted the junk yard which loomed in the semi-moonlight. She halted high above it and gently floated down towards the familiar heaps of rusty car bodies and twisted sheets of metal. This is the junkyard near Dad's factory after all, she concluded. She felt a little more comforted knowing she was back somewhere familiar. She suddenly felt sleepy and laughed to herself that this was a ridiculous thing for a ghost to do – sleep. But it was not the kind of sleep to dream and be lost forever. She somehow knew this, as this kind of drowsiness felt more relaxing, in a way. Confounded, she felt her eyelids sag as her form settled into the cracked-leather back seat of an old Studebaker. She instantly felt safe but couldn't figure out why, as a strange kind of warmth enveloped her relaxed form and it felt as if someone was resting a blanket around her.

Memories can be strong, she pondered. She could think of all the simple comforts she enjoyed while alive and they somehow felt true even now she was dead. She wondered what Zane was doing right now and suddenly feared the Munchers might find him, but the strange unthreatening drowsiness took hold of her and she drifted in and out of a semi-doze. She edged her eyes open every now and then to remind herself that consciousness would keep her alert enough to flee from the Munchers should they come in the night. She gazed up into the night sky and spotted a small light high overhead. She assured herself it was just an airplane, as more images of her living past floated before her, the last image in her mind a more recent event – the strange man emerging from a pool of glistening, dancing light. At that, she fell asleep.

* * *

A metallic clanging caused Angela to spring awake. Something moved outside and her heart leapt when a large chocolate-colored Labrador lunged into the car and decided to take rest where she had slept.

"Get out!" she yelled at the top of her voice.

The dog's ears instantly pricked up.

"Get outta here!" she yelled again.

The dog whimpered and lunged off the car seat, scampering away. Angela peeked outside and noticed the sun was setting. "I've been asleep all day!" she gasped.

"Ghosts need sleep too," a voice boomed in the distance.

"What? Who?" Angela rubbed her eyes and blinked.

"I can *see-e-e* you," rang the voice in a childish tone. It was a hollow voice that rattled off the corrugated metal sheets leaning haphazardly against the mounds of cars. But it was the voice of an adult.

Angela narrowed her eyes as something flashed in the distance but couldn't stop a smile forcing her cheeks to bulge. She suddenly felt safe again, safe like returning to her family after a long adventure away somewhere. But this person was not family, though he could be the only closest being in this eternal death zone who took notice. She flung her spirit through the blistered roof of the car and headed for the familiar friend who stood waiting with an even bigger smile.

The Chronokey

13: The Dumpster Man

"So, you have found me again, or perhaps I found you?" The Dumpster Man's face wrinkled with delight as Angela approached, zigzagging through the piles of junk in his yard.

"So you *did* bring me here," she said. "How'd you do it?"

"Oh not I," he said, shaking his head. "Not this time. There must be children nearby."

"Huh?"

"Kid ghosts, *kidred* spirits you could say. You're drawn to them, you and him," he said with a sigh. "Similar souls have a habit of homing in on each other."

"You've met other kids then, kids like—" she stopped short, wondering if the Dumpster Man knew about the students from Spook School.

"They come and go," he said lightly. "Nobody stays here forever. Who'd want to? Except me, of course; I love this kind of place. The whole world will be like this one day."

Angela tried to push such a thought out of her mind – the whole world a junk yard like this – but her immediate surroundings of rusted car bodies, broken washing machines and unrecognizable contraptions clapping their metal doors in the breeze were too much. "The human race makes so much rubbish," she commented. "So you really like this place, eh? Couldn't be anything to do with my father's factory nearby?"

The Dumpster Man jumped off a stack of tires and stared at her evenly. "Maybe … and maybe not." The pile of tires swayed from his weight as he pushed away from them. He dusted himself and grinned, rubbing his hands together. "But it's good to see you again!" He waved a finger. "You know, your father was a brilliant man."

"Yeah, was," she said glumly. "All we've got is his junk and you—"

"I know, I know," he said trying to hush her. "Not even I know where he is for sure – but he'll be alright." He winked. "Just you see."

"You said that before," she said glumly.

Angela thought he was a little simple, but the kinds of gadgets she saw him build looked complex, and she couldn't figure out what they were used for, except perhaps for one panel with a big display of colored worms intertwining, expanding and contracting.

The Dumpster Man stood in muddy soil, not giving a care as he probed the pockets in his stained denim overalls. "Not there... no not there... Ah." He produced a scrappy piece of paper. "Did you find him? Did he dream or is he awake?"

"Oh," Angela turned away. "Why are you so interested in *him*? What's so special about him anyway?"

"If he's dreaming," he said slowly, "he'll be lost."

"He won't," Angela said. "I know it."

"But if he stays in one place, they'll find him and *eat* him."

"Oh, the Munchers," Angela said. "I hung around in that car for a while and I'm still here."

The Dumpster Man leaned forward, tilting his head with an intense gaze and emphasis on his words, "That's different; that's *sleeping*. Tell me, child, is he awake?"

"How's that different?"

The Dumpster Man forced his words. "Is he *awake*?"

"Yes," Angela said solemnly. "Last time I saw him." She eyed him carefully. "But so are you."

"Hah-hah!" The Dumpster Man rocked with laughter, almost knocking over the stack of tires beside him. He stretched the elastic braces of his overalls, releasing them to slap against his chest. "You're smarter than you look, girl, or is that... prettier than you think? No-no... that's not right." He paused and considered his phrasing. "Ah, no matter, you're cleverer than I think! Yes indeed, oh indeed yes!"

Angela folded her arms. She didn't know if he was stalling or simply behaving like an overgrown child. "You can see me, because you're dead," she said flatly.

"But I'm *alive*," he said smiling.

"You're dead, deady-dead!" Angela blurted.

"Maybe, and maybe not. Can a mortal see the dead? Ah! Don't answer that, because you see, I could be alive too!"

Angela scratched her head. "Huh? How can a dead man be alive? Besides—" She suddenly stared at the tires, the way they swayed as he leaned against them. She watched his boots swill the muddy ground. Things are moving, she thought. Matter is moving.

The Dumpster Man raised his finger and a brow. "Ah, you see?" He patted his chest. "I'm solid!"

"But you're *dead!*" Angela insisted. "How'd you do this? Have you got back to life?"

He pulled at the scraggly hairs on his chin, his smile giving way to perplexity. "No... err, yes... but certain particulars are beyond me right now..."

"Well, which is it?"

His expression dropped. "Oh, never you mind about that right now."

"Never I mind?" her face turned red. "You ask me about him, as if you didn't know…"

"What's that?"

She folded her arms and looked him squarely in the face. "…Jesus!"

The Dumpster Man rubbed a chin bristling with stray hairs. "Jesus? Jesus Christ?"

"Don't mess with me," Angela scorned, "I saw you in the time machine. You were him, though with less hair on your head—"

"Uh-huh—"

"And you were somewhat more confident, intelligent—"

"Oh," he chuckled, scratching the back of his head, "why, thank you," and then his smile dropped and he tilted his head with curiosity. "No wait a minute… you think you saw *me* – in a time machine? Tell me about the machine," he said slowly, rubbing his bristles.

Angela gulped and thought perhaps she hadn't seen the Dumpster Man after all. She stood her ground. "I'm not saying any more. Just don't mess with me, you!"

"I can only mess so far," he said with open arms. He sighed and leaned against the stack of tires.

Her arms dropped to her side and she tilted her head in confusion. "So if you're not posing as Jesus, then who—"

The Dumpster Man snapped his fingers. "My brother! Curse his soul... or is that bless his soul? Oh, what a wit, incredibly daring. Oh, what nerve!"

"*You* have a brother? Another like you?"

"Bah! Not like me, he's a complete, calculating megalomaniac. He loves to role play the big names. We were separated at birth ... let's see... a long time from now... hmm!" He scratched a thick eyebrow and nodded with knowing astonishment. "So long, so long ago... tomorrow..."

"Huh?" she flicked back her straggling fringe. Her face creased with profound perplexity. "You're so ridiculous!"

He waved his hands before her. "Oh calm down my confounded missy. I didn't know I had a brother, only to bump into him at the point of death, which told me also that I had been around a lot longer than I had..."

She rolled her eyes. "I give up."

"Oh,"– he waved his hand dismissively – "that's another long story... attached to another story...attached to another..."

214

Angela folded her arms in frustration. "And he can travel in time, this brother?"

"In a manner of thinking, err, speaking," the Dumpster Man said slowly. "And I can, too," he boasted. "I just..." – he sighed again – "I just don't have all the mislaid pieces for complete autonomy and am now stuck here. Oh, of course, I could seek help from him but, oh, I'm too proud for that."

Angela became more confused as she swung her near-transparent foot through the muddy soil to no effect. "Who... or *what* are you, anyway? You go back further in time, don't you? Are you human at all? What's with your brother coming in and saving us back in the time box?"

"How should I know, child? My, we're plucky and confused, aren't we?"

Angela flicked her fringe away from her eyes again, feeling annoyed by this permanent fixture on her ghostly form. Her face then filled with a look of disgust. "How could a guy pose as Jesus, just to take advantage of people, even if it's well-intended? Those people in the time machine – they made that machine and they're mortal like me."

The Dumpster Man raised a finger. "Well actually you're—"

"And how," Angela interjected, "did Jesus or whatever he is get in there, anyway?"

The Dumpster Man shook his head as he tried to hold back a laugh. "Bless him. Curse him, what courage! Humankind is right to a degree. We gods do like our sport."

"Call yourself a god? It's pathetic."

"But you, my child, you are—"

"Stop it!" Angela swung away from him.

The Dumpster Man touched her shoulder and for a moment his touch made her shoulder feel like solid matter. She shuddered and edged further away.

"I'm so sorry, child," he said with a soft smile. "You're not much older than he is." A look of concern suddenly crossed his face. "Speaking of which, why'd you leave him?"

"Leave Zane?"

"I'm going to have to use the funnel scope to map you back there."

"The funnel what?" she asked in a moment of curiosity – curiosity that again quickly gave place to obstinacy. "Why's he so important?" she asked defiantly. "And who are you to want to contact a complete stranger?"

"Like I contacted you?" The Dumpster man said quietly.

Angela gulped again.

"Not many survive the bridge," he said.

"The bridge?"

"The moment between life and death. Sometimes I stumble upon souls at the point of death because their life essences cry out into the night like the lights of Vegas—"

Angela shrieked, "The burning feeling!"

"That's the one," he said. "It's your energy tearing into a new dimension. I got to you in time, dear. Remember the Munchers? If they were around they would have ripped you away into the void and possibly through a fading dream. That moment from death's delirium to post-life consciousness is the most dangerous one." He sighed. "You are right, I am not a god and who on earth would want a trash lord? And, as such, I cannot be everywhere at the same time unless the essence of diffusion is—" He stopped and drummed his lip. "Ah, I do go on."

He heaved a heavy sigh and smiled crookedly, tapping his nose as he squinted into her curious brown-green eyes. "You know our friend; I imparted some wake up lines to kind of keep him alert and safe from sleep."

"*You* did that?" She glared at him with narrowing eyes. "He talks of crazy poems in his head. Was that you?"

The Dumpster Man stammered, "I … err ... well, just a little tome machine, that's all."

"A bad tome machine, no doubt."

The Dumpster Man grabbed his braces again and chuckled lightly. "Well, I think I mastered it quite well. I didn't need a tome machine for you; your death, err… was made more traumatic by the recent loss of your father. It kept you well awake and, so far, you haven't become obsessed by it. And as for the other children out there..."

She again turned away from his fat face and curious blue-eyed gaze. "You never told me your real name," she said sullenly.

"Phil," he said proudly. "Phil the lackey who used to pump gas. 'Phil 'er up here'– he waved his arm in the air – 'Phil 'er up there'... you know how it is."

"No I don't," Angela said with a look of disdain on her face. "I think your brother is nicer and I'm sure he saw me."

"I think he's seen you twice," Phil said quietly. "And he's not always nice."

"What?"

"Oh, yes. He doesn't always look the same, you know?"

Angela's thoughts coursed through all the events that had taken place up till then – all the places they had visited, the people she had encountered and watched with silence and wonder. She concentrated hard and felt she knew who it was, but it slipped away. Then, as the sun set on a jagged pile of car bodies in the distance, she spotted it. A gray overcoat lay slumped over a mangled car door. Hanging from the pocket was a long, chunky chain. Nothing else protruded from the pocket but light – multicolored light. She gulped and took a step back, now knowing at last who she was dealing with.

14: Home

Zane spirited away from the Principal's office, feeling satisfied that Higgins was finally being disciplined, even though he could almost believe Higgins's sob story that he wasn't there at all when it happened. He makes for a convincing liar, Zane mused. It was a basketball that knocked Alfred over, that's all. But Zane knew better. He flew high above the school grounds, pleased that Higgins would be on detention and schoolyard maintenance for three months. But somehow that wasn't enough punishment.

He scoped the area below and tracked his eyes along a major highway leading away from the school, guessing Alfred would be taken to the main city hospital. He was keen to get to Alfred, to speak with him again. But when he spotted the hospital buildings in the distance, he gulped, knowing his mother's house was on the way. His heart leapt with a mix of sadness and excitement. Drop in quickly before reaching Alfred, see what they're doing. They won't see me, he assured himself, but at least I can see if they're getting on. Maybe I'll feel more at ease then.

He swung low and sifted his spirit through the trees. It felt soothing to feel something less impacting than brick, though more solid than air, dart through his being; the crimson leaves felt more like the wind against his face and reminded him of the days when he used to ride pillion on Dad's motorbike. He spotted his home in the distance and approached hesitantly, wondering if perhaps he shouldn't know what is happening in his family now. He could be nothing but a memory a million miles away from any current concern, away in mind, up in the sky or heaven or wherever they may think he is. People like to compartmentalize everyday aspects, even the ethereal.

He hovered low over Jennifer's bedroom window and noticed the garden below was mowed, the leaves of fall raked to one side. This was not the way he saw his house in Mister Numan's world. Things felt alive and fresh and Zane was sure he could smell a scent from the garden wafting his way. He looked into Jennifer's bedroom but she was not there. He guessed she must be on her way home from school by now. He seeped through the wall and casually floated down the stairs. This was, after all his home and the feelings of being home were welcoming.

Mom stood at the bottom of the stairs, holding the phone. "Yes, large supreme without olives."

Pizza? Zane scratched his head. We only got pizza when Dad was around. And it's too early for dinner.

A rattle of keys at the front door told Zane that Jenny was home. She heaved the door open and brushed her way past her mother. "Kate's guinea pig died. I have to go over there to bury it."

"But I've just ordered dinner!" Mom protested.

"Gotta bury it now, before it stinks," Jennifer said.

"Why can't Kate do it?"

"Sorry, Mom," Jennifer sighed, "Kate says I'm more experienced with things dying."

"I see," Mom said quietly. "What about dinner?"

"Okay," Jennifer huffed, looking up to the ceiling, all wide-eyed and open-mouthed. "Let's see, Thursday. It's supreme pizza again. Mom, you know I hate olives."

"No olives, dear."

"Can't we have something different? Anyway, Kate's mom is having roast."

Mom fell back on the small telephone chair and sighed. "Okay, dear." she brushed aside an annoying length of curly dark hair, a length of gray at the roots showing in the dim light of the entrance hall. "I'll pick you up in three hours."

"Earth to mother, I'm thirteen now. I can get myself home," she said.

"Not when so many children have been disappearing at night," she said. "I don't want you to be another missing person statistic."

Jennifer groaned and raced up the stairs to her bedroom, dropping her school books on the way. She stopped abruptly and stood frozen at the top of the landing, staring blankly at the wall.

Zane froze where he floated. For a moment Jennifer was staring at him, right at his eyes. He hovered back a little and she blinked, took a step down and gathered her books.

A sudden barking cut through the silence as Mitch slammed through the pet door in the kitchen. Zane could hear the little paws skittle across the kitchen tiles then thud onto the carpet, as Mitch dashed up the stairs, almost causing Jennifer to drop her books again. Mitch stopped sharply before Zane, ears cocked and tail wagging furiously. He barked incessantly and sniffed the air. Zane could see the little dog was excited more than spooked and wondered if all this was because of his presence.

"Mitch!" Jennifer protested. "What's with you?"

Mitch continued to bark and Zane slipped back through the frosted stained window nearby to hover outside. He squinted to see back through the orange bubble glass. Mitch had calmed down, sitting on the carpet, still wagging his tail and staring in Zane's direction.

Zane wondered what it was about dogs; perhaps they are more intuitive and that would explain why some things unseen by humans often spook dogs into erratic behavior. But it didn't explain how Alfred could have seen him and, for a moment, did Jen see him or was that a book-dropping coincidence? Zane began to wonder if his presence here would be a constant upset. Perhaps he should go and see how Alfred was getting on. He looked back at Mitch, the poor little Jack Russell, wide eyes glistening in the hall light and his head tilted, almost expecting Zane to melt through the window to greet him.

Zane tried to piece together the puzzling images of his death, as being here reminded him more of his own death than anything else. He gazed on the little dog pawing the air.

"I think I got killed saving you," he mumbled. "Killed..."

Mitch gave a single searching bark.

"Yes!" Zane gasped, "I saved your butt, little buddy. Well I think I did." He tried to grasp more of the memory that was just beyond reach but it faded, but for the shrill of barking, the tight and throaty retching from the neighbor's slobbery bulldog. "A dog fight?" Zane asked himself. "How could I die from that?" His eyes remained fixed upon the little creature and he guessed Mitch felt some kind of guilt. "Of course you do," he said softly. "I remember when you whimpered after I scolded you for swiping my sandwiches, and the time you crapped in my schoolbag..."

Zane suddenly felt silly and glumly realized that perhaps Angela was right. A slight mistake or just a little turn of events could cut life off so quickly without warning.

He gazed longingly at the small creature, wanting to hold him again but not wanting to cause a disturbance. But I can't hold you now, he thought sadly. He nodded slightly and a warm feeling filled his transparent being, forcing him to smile like an adult does – not a grin, but a smile that says a lot without saying anything. At least knowing he saved a life was enough. "And I'd do it again if I were given a second go at life," he said softly to the gazing animal.

Mitch gave another single loud bark, as if to acknowledge him.

Jennifer crouched beside Mitch and stared at the frozen glass. "What's with you, anyway? You miss

Zane, don't you? He was a pain in the ass sometimes with his stinkin' this and stinkin' that, but I miss him too, Mitch – a lot."

Mitch glanced at her quickly and returned his gaze at the glass. He somehow knew Zane was outside and Zane felt a strange combination of feeling at ease and unsettled at the same time.

Zane smiled the kind of smile that was lost and longing and he wanted to embrace both of them. He watched Jennifer go up the short flight of steps and down the corridor to her bedroom. She called to Mitch who stopped every yard or so to glance back at the window on the landing.

"C'mon, silly," Jennifer called.

Zane swung around the outside of the house towards Jen's bedroom, stopping short to glance down at the kitchen. Mom was wiping the kitchen bench tops. Everything looked normal until Zane spotted a tear trail down her left cheek. This is not good, he thought. They've got to let go.

Then it was his turn. The glistening transparent orb of a tear pushed its way through the corner of his right eye. "This is not good for any of us," he said softly.

* * *

Jake Numan kicked the loose stones that had broken away from the sidewalk outside the cemetery. A longer way home, he thought, but a nice way to go, if he wanted to be near his old buddy Zane and glimpse his resting place from afar. He thought about stopping and seeing Zane's stone up close but couldn't bring himself to go any closer.

"Ouch!" He stubbed his toe over a section of path that had cracked and lifted. He remembered his Dad complaining to the council about the state of the sidewalk but their only reply was they'd get around to it when they could. Dad had told him the council had no money because it all went to the damn lawyers fighting ugly developments in the area. Jake knew better. The cemetery had a history of sorts, with all kinds of weird things happening to those visiting for any length of time. A road works crew persisted with path maintenance and curbing, until finally being scared away by too many accidents. He remembered locals talking about the cement truck incident a few months ago. The truck was said to have rolled and killed a workmate but the handbrake was on and the gear left in Park.

Yet all that crap shouldn't bother me, Jake thought, not at all while Zane's in there. He spotted Zane's area beyond the larger headstones that had tilted from the work of restless tree roots, spanning some two hundred years of growth. Then he spied someone crouching down near Zane's grave, a grown-up. He stopped and clasped the wrought iron fence, wondering who it could be.

He's leaning over Zane's grave. Who is he?

Jake looked back along the path and realized it was too far back to the main entrance he had passed earlier. He heaved his school sack over the iron fence and jumped after it. He dusted his bag and casually wandered into the cemetery, emerging through the trees to get a better look.

Coming back so soon after Zane's death was unnerving but he felt determined to find out who the stranger was. He headed for the gravestones just beyond Zane's grave where the stranger was now standing and looking down upon Zane's plot. Jake casually strolled behind him and the man didn't swing to look. Jake crouched down in front of another grave. He stared blankly at the stone before him but carefully glanced through the corner of his eye at the man stooped over Zane's grave. The man's left cheek glinted in the afternoon light, perhaps from a slight tear.

The man glanced at Jake then looked away.

Jake's heart leapt when the man looked at him again. He was familiar in a way though a little shabby, his clothes pock-marked by holes. The man wove his fingers through a short, scraggly beard and then turned to look at Jake.

Jake stood up awkwardly and stepped back.

"No fun coming to a place like this," the man said with a dry voice.

Jake stepped back further. "Suppose," he gulped.

The man stooped to look at the stone before Jake. "Ah, you know Warwick Numan?"

"I... err," Jake looked again at the stone which read, *'Here lies Warwick Numan, Father of Peter Joseph Numan'*. Jake hadn't realized he was standing before his grandfather's stone, but it made sense as their families were close. He wondered why he hadn't come here before but guessed he was too young when his grandfather died and nobody in the family would talk about his grandfather – in particular his Dad. Jake always wondered if there was something that tore them apart in the past but he guessed he'd never know now. He felt a little comforted knowing Zane was buried in good company and realized he was too distraught at the funeral to take in any of the surroundings.

"Good 'ol Warwick. I used to play with his son, Pete," the stranger said, "when I was a boy; you a friend of the family?"

Jake felt a little uneasy at the man's attention and looked back at his grandfather's stone. "I'm Jake Numan."

"Pete's son? Well, that's great!" His face lit up and he instantly appeared several years younger. He stretched out a worn and grubby hand. "I'm Simon Carter."

Jake gulped. "Zane's du-dad? Here?" He kicked the gravel, his voice beginning to stammer, "W-why... now? I mean, you've come back—"

"Too late?"

"Well... yeah!" Jake couldn't contain himself. He thought the guy had looked familiar and if this really was Zane's father then he has changed a ton for the worse.

Simon Carter cleared his throat. "Sorry, that came out wrong. I... perhaps I should accompany you back home."

"No, sorry, I gotta go," Jake said hurriedly. He picked up his feet to run, uncertain of what to do but run, nonetheless; it was the only thing that came to mind. Zane's mom will shit herself, he thought.

"Stop!" yelled Mister Carter. "I'm going now; you can stay. You can say goodbye or hello or whatever to Zane. It's okay."

Jake stopped abruptly and dropped his school sack. He about-faced slowly and saw that Mister Carter was gone, as if he had just vanished. He kicked the gravel aside and trudged back to Zane's grave, glancing around on occasion to catch a glimpse of the departing Mister Carter. But the man had left swiftly without as much as a shoe impression in the path.

Jake looked at Zane's grave and frowned. "Fancy your Dad coming here after all this time. What a Waldo and he stinks. He's so different. Must be the beard but he looks run down. My dad ain't much, but at least he didn't shoot off without so much as a 'thank ya, see ya later'."

Jake looked down and bit his lower lip. "Sorry pal. That was outta line. Say, you know Alfred got beat up by Higgins today and Higgins got busted big time. Alfred's in hospital because of that fat bitch ass. Higgins'll pay for sure."

Jake suddenly looked up and around the graveyard. He felt a little uneasy and lowered his voice, "Zane, I feel a bit dumb talking to a lump of stone and knowing you're a bunch of rottin' bones a few feet down, but heck, why should I care? I miss you buddy. I miss your jokes and stinkin' this and stinkin' that. We all miss you." He heaved his school sack onto his back and with his shoe smoothed over some of the loosened gravel he had kicked before. "Stay cool; hey, what else can you do now?"

At that he turned and left.

Within the foliage of an aged beech tree nearby, a pair of narrow, bloodshot eyes watched Jake Numan depart from Zane's grave. A haughty dry whisper sounded through the flittering leaves in a breeze now picking up, "Soon your friend will be with *me*."

15: The Watch

"Abaddon's your brother!" Angela said wide-eyed. "He's the Devil! Satan!"

"Oh, come now, child; not Satan," said the Dumpster Man in dulcet tones. He then pointed a shaky finger at her, his voice now terse. "But a devil you wouldn't want to cross, that be for sure. Unless," he paused, rubbing his chin, "you get him on a good millennium err… day."

"You've both got those strange watches with lots of hands and buttons and glowing lights," she said.

"Well, in a sense," he chuckled. "His is the real thing; mine's just a cheap Omega, if you know what I mean."

"Not quite."

"Well I didn't manage to obtain all the plans and, when I did, he messed it up for me, but don't trouble yourself over it, child."

"What do they do?"

"Ah, anything and everything. A compact lifeometer, well, ahem, his is, anyway."

"Lifeometer?"

"A device to measure life, its bounds and deathly energies beyond – a device that transmutes matter, can travel to it or from it. However," his voice lowered, "it was only intended for corporeal time travel but something went fantastically wrong."

Bewildered, Angela leaned against an open car door which seemed to acknowledge her by creaking back in the wind to let her slump on the faded and cracked upholstery.

"It's too much for you, isn't it, dear," The Dumpster Man said. He leaned over her, his grease-smeared frown intensifying. "Give it time." He about-faced and headed for an old weather-beaten building made out of loosely-fitted tin sheeting.

"But—" Angela stopped. She wondered if she should ask him about Spook School, to learn about the afterlife, perhaps to learn to move on from here to wherever. But she hated school. She hated the way they all picked on her. She wondered if the Dumpster Man knew the Gatherer.

Something touched her ear, causing it to flex. She could hear him singing from within the shabby building...

"My name is Doctor Worm," he sung in a hollow voice, "I'm not a real doctor but I am a real worm, a fuzzy little worm..." The shack resonated to his voice, the overlaps of corrugated sheeting rattling from his disturbing, child-like song. For a moment she thought he was the most ridiculous thing she had met in this afterlife.

She struggled up from the rusted hulk of a car she had slumped into. It was quite comfortable in the late afternoon sun but now it was getting cold. She thought to herself, I'm not cold, it's only my perception. I'm a ghost, I am. The feeling of comfort returned and she realized she felt all sorts of things, often at once, and this was the most unsettling feeling of all. She began to wonder just how human, just how real she really was.

She sprang upright and yelled, "Wait! I need to know more!" She leaped out beyond the car and flew into the tin shack, suddenly feeling the impact of knowing that matter can be moved by a kind of non-matter. The Dumpster Man could walk and make footprints in the grease-laced soil. She had to know how to do it.

"How do I move things?" she yelled.

"In time, dear child," he said, distracted. "You are one of the first in the short history of the universe – you and Zane – and some others."

"First of what?"

"A new breed of consciousness," he said with his back to her, "A new ghost." He leaned over the machine she had spotted earlier.

Angela mulled over the weird instrumentation and glowing dials on the Dumpster Man's console. She then eyed the watch hanging over the open car door in the distance, swinging gently on its chain in a breeze that was picking up.

The Dumpster man caught her gaze and spoke with his head down over the glowing monitor, "Apart from the box, there are only two watches I know of, my brother's and mine," he paused, then his voice went gruff with dissatisfaction, "and his is working properly, too."

"What box?"

He slammed an open hand against the side of the machine. "Silly contraption! If I only had some more energy."

Angela stepped back, surprised at his change in tone. "Where did they come from? You made them?"

The Dumpster Man's ignored her question, but his smile returned. "Speaking of time, it's time to get you back to Zane, my dear, and fast – if he stays there, he'll be taken."

"But—"

"Forget the watch, dear child. Zane cannot persist in the same place, you know."

"Just why can't a person hang around in the same place?" Angela asked. "Why do we have to move all the time? Why can't we stand our ground? Why do they come to take us?"

The Dumpster man chuckled. "Munchers, you could say, are the cleaners of the afterlife. But there are other dangers..." He frowned. "It is a sad fact of conscious death that, if you want to stay self-aware in the afterlife, you have to be on your glowing little toes, alert at all times, or," he waved a finger, "know how to sleep in such a way as to keep a foothold on your reality. It is a deep sleep, beyond the realm of dreams, and I think, my child, you may get the knack of it."

"It wasn't you who protected me then?" she asked.

"Me?" He flashed a smile. "If you think so child; if you think so."

"Hmm," she moaned.

"I – I do have a machine that can warn of their approach but they don't come here very often."

On a rusty panel he heaved a large knife switch to the down position. Old fashioned incandescent lights, covered under years of dust, blinked on to glow a soft yellow haze.

"I met some kids who said they were protected from Munchers," Angela blurted.

"Oh, yes," – The Dumpster Man raised one eyebrow, dismissing her comment – "guided by fools no doubt, fools you don't want to mess with."

A burst of sparks came from the side of the machine, blasting a panel through the air in a gush of smoke and cinders. The panel clanged on the concrete floor, skimming across the room to hit the opposite wall.

"Oh, blasted thing," he cursed. He stuck his head inside the contraption and waved his hand through the air as if to clear the smoke, even though it partly wafted through him. What didn't waft through him turned and weaved in the air in little circles as he motioned with his arm. He ripped out a cable and Angela watched, gawk-eyed, amazed at how a ghost could manipulate matter so easily.

He glanced at her amazement and winked. "This machine is not all matter, you know, even though you can see it."

"Then what is it, if it's not all there?"

"Well you're not all here!" he said laughing. "And," – he tickled his chin – "I'm not all here either! Must ask my shrink about that one day." He dusted his hands and walked to another machine, the strange scope

Angela had spotted earlier. "Matter is multi-dimensional," he said. "Some of it you can see and touch. A lot of it you can't. It's all about phasing."

"I see," she said quietly.

"Of course you do, child," he chuckled. "Of course you do."

Angela's curiosity was taken by the Dumpster Man's motions over the strange scope. He flicked two switches and rested his hand on a control that looked like an arcade game joystick control. Colored trails flowed across the display and, as he moved the joystick, a flashing crosshatch skimmed across the screen. He released the stick when the crosshatch began to flash faster.

He glanced at her curious face and smiled. "Funnel map, in essence," he said. "If my watch worked properly it would do splendidly; however, this junky pastiche will have to suffice. We'll find a funnel that'll lead to Zane, don't you worry. Funnels move, but can be tracked."

"How come they're colored on the screen?"

"The funnels? Oh well, this machine can see their full spectrum. But if you looked hard, you too could see some colors in them." He sighed. "Ghosts always seem to see them in shades of gray."

Angela examined the machine more closely. Mashed together were a strange array of old hardware and some odd shiny lengths of metal that appeared to ripple in the light. One side of the contraption was splashed in carnival-like colors, and she guessed that part of the machine originated from a carnival or arcade game house. A giant frog squashed by a truck tire was painted across the side of the machine. She didn't recognize the name of the game, *Interstate Frogger*. Then she spotted some familiar components mounted under the display screen, lots of glowing numbers and some unfamiliar characters flashing in unison. They were similar to those seen in Niva's time cube. Her eyes widened when she recognized the displays. They were displays made in her father's factory, displays that should have been junked as they had tested faulty; the word 'fail' was etched on them. This man has got them working. This man knows a lot, she mused. That knowledge hidden beneath his polite and almost child-like eccentricities made her feel a little uncomfortable.

"Just who are you, anyway?" she asked. Then she felt herself compelled to ask, "And just how *old* are you?"

"Now child, it is a little impolite to ask an elder his age, no?"

"Hundreds of years?" she asked.

The Dumpster Man rocked with laugher. "Depends on how you measure time. But we digress, don't we? Look at the scope, child."

Angela hovered over the Dumpster Man's shoulder to see the colored array of funnels intertwining themselves on the display.

"Funnel maps run in real time," he said. "If they didn't, if they were even a millisecond out, then you could be lost. I have calibrated it to the watch stream and all we have to do is home in on Zane. You saw him last at his school in Century City?"

"Yes," Angela said with curiosity. Her head glowed with the rainbow of colors radiating from the monitor. "But what if he has moved on from there? Or if a Muncher chases him away?"

"It's the best I can do," The Dumpster Man replied with a sigh. "If my watch was fully functional I could take you there without the aid of a funnel, but, alas, it was damaged by my brother in our last encounter. The best I can do is to home in on Zane's grave. Ah," he clapped his hands, "a suitable one is in our vicinity. See that light?" He pointed to a flashing light dangling off a wire that appeared to be partly ripped out from the console.

Angela suddenly began to feel a little uncertain about the accuracy of this machine.

He then tapped the crosshatch on the monitor. It flashed rapidly. "They tell us one is near, the right one for you."

"But—"

"Up there," The Dumpster Man pointed. "Right above us it swirls. Go, child, go now!"

Angela looked up and gulped. The funnel was darker than any she had entered before. "Sure this goes to Zane's?" she asked.

"Yes child, and do not worry about its shade. There can be more light in the foamy dark than we could ever dream of."

Angela tilted her head in confusion and Phil gave a slight chuckle.

She suddenly asked, "So why can't you go into a funnel?"

"Oh?" he chuckled and slapped his belly. "Too heavy, oh my, yes, a legacy of tampering with matter. Go now, child, and do not be afraid."

Angela could do nothing but go. She quickly thought about going back the way she came but as The Dumpster Man said, funnels change all the time. If she knew the address of Zane Carter, at least his graveyard, if she could only find her way back along a more traditional way, across hundreds of miles of countryside, then she'd do it. But right now, this was her only chance to get back to Zane, and perhaps steer him away from sudden danger. She looked up at the funnel entrance misting and swaying in the sky above. It thrashed and coiled like a whip as if to prompt her and she glanced at Phil the Dumpster Man with an uncertain face. He motioned her to get a move on.

"'Bye then," she said solemnly. She quickly embraced him and felt all the matter she used to feel when she was held by her father. She gave a hurried smile and instantly shifted into her glowing shapeless form to shoot upwards at high speed, disappearing into the dark cloudy mass of the funnel.

She watched the funnel exit close behind her, the ground below rotating as the funnel sucked her form further into its snakelike coils. The funnel buffeted her as she felt drawn towards its exit, a short trip that made her feel uneasy, sensing a magnetic-like pull on her form as if something else was in the funnel with her. She rounded a corner expecting the exit as the funnel filled with a cotton-like mist. The exit was sudden and harsh, bursting her through a thickened wall; she tried to glance back at the mouth of the funnel but couldn't see it. She coughed from what felt like smoke and covered her eyes as she slowed to hover in cloudless sky, a now brighter daylight sky. She glided over the city of headstones jutting out below her.

I'm back, she thought, but I'll never get used to the changes in day and night between different areas. She spied the gravestones below but something was wrong. The graveyard appeared different from the one she met Zane in. Stones appeared more elegant, individually fenced by wrought iron. Her heart suddenly leapt and for a moment she thought she saw the little orb of light that was her heart shoot from her glowing chest in a racing panic.

"This place is wrong," she said, flinging her anxious gaze around the strange cemetery. "This is the wrong graveyard!"

16: Hospital Exits

Zane spotted the grey mass of the hospital in the distance, a grid of lights that appeared as a guiding beacon in the now darkening sky. Funnels snaked through the clouds above and Zane wondered if he should funnel exit out of there after seeing Alfred, but Angela might come back and he wasn't ready to leave just yet.

He sailed down through the brightly-lit emergency entrance and wondered how ridiculous it would be for a ghost to ask reception where to visit a patient. This time he is going to have to find Alfred himself if it meant he had to seep through every wall and floor to find the right ward. At least there was a good chance he'd still be in the emergency wing somewhere. Then the most disturbing thought entered his mind: whether he'd encounter the freshly dead – those patients exuding en masse from where they died. But this wasn't a terminating hospital and hopefully there shouldn't be any hordes of scared ghosts to push him out of their way.

Zane hovered over several patients. Some groaned in torn agony, their faces bloodied and almost shapeless from what he guessed could have been a major accident on the interstate, as doctors and nurses hurriedly wheeled their patients to theater. The voices of panic filled the wing and, for a moment, Zane quivered from the impact of a foreign thought touching the edge of his mind, an image of a semi-trailer skidding sideways and hurtling towards him. He blinked hard and swung about to try to catch where the dread had come from. He looked at each mangled patient but it was difficult in the deafening melee around him. That fleeting thought came from one of the injured, Zane knew for sure, and he understood then that his mind could catch the sharp spikes of thoughts around him, maybe the thoughts of those on the precipice of death.

He quivered again and slipped through a wall into another wing and then entered a ward where some children were propped up to eat their dinners. Alfred was not here and Zane left immediately, feeling a little queasy at the sight of people eating when he could not. He felt a sensation of familiar memories, a growling filled his tummy area, and what felt like the remains of a phantom tongue tingled with the thought of frozen yoghurt.

He slipped back through the wall into another ward containing older people, passing through an oscilloscope that appeared to announce his presence by offering a few rapid beeps, causing a nurse to check the instrument and feel a sleeping man's pulse. Zane wondered if perhaps that monitor picked up his energy pulse or something. He spotted another corridor leading from this ward and carefully zigzagged his way past patients and heart monitors. Then he found the isolation ward.

Couldn't be in there, he thought, but he poked his head through the door anyway, just to see who was in there. Resting alone beside a bank of monitors and coiled wires was Alfred.

"I can't believe it," said a voice from behind.

Zane shuddered as a doctor walked through him, entering the room with a nurse. He still wasn't comfortable about living matter moving through him.

The doctor leaned over Alfred and took his pulse, and then he lifted the bandage from across Alfred's forehead.

The nurse's eyes widened. "Impossible!"

Zane floated over the pair of them and looked down upon Alfred. He couldn't believe it himself. A few hours ago Alfred was covered in bruises and had a gash across his forehead. Now most of the injuries appeared to have healed, but for a slight blue tinge across his face.

"Get his parents back here," the doctor ordered.

"But they've just left," the nurse replied.

"I need to ask them a few questions," the doctor said quickly, and then added, "and maybe take their blood samples as well."

"What's going on?" the nurse asked.

"That's what I want to find out," the doctor said as he probed the room for a syringe. "He has shown incredibly rapid healing."

The nurse hurried into the corridor and moments later returned with Alfred's parents.

"Right, sorry to bring you back so quickly," he said to Alfred's parents. "I was wondering if I could take your blood samples also."

"What is it, doctor?" Alfred's mother asked.

Zane felt relieved Alfred's parents were here and instantly wondered if the same care and attention would be directed to him if his Mom and Dad were around. Silly, he thought, of course Mom, at least, would come to see me.

Zane watched the loving attention of Alfred's mother as she stroked her son's head with amazement on her face.

"It's happened sooner than we thought," she said quietly to her husband.

Alfred's father, a tall man with almost no hair on his head and unusually small ears, nodded slightly as the doctor called the nurse back into the room.

"Excuse me, doctor, but I really must protest at having my blood taken," said Alfred's father, his eyes quite wide – a deep green-brown glinting in the harsh fluorescents.

"Oh, but we must," The doctor said.

A loud repetitious beep uttered from the ward next door. A flurry of nurses and a doctor raced past them.

"Back in a minute," the doctor said.

Zane hovered around the ward, wondering what the hell was going on. Then he heard Alfred's waking voice. "Zane! You're here."

"Quiet, darling," said his mother.

Zane stared at him and wondered how someone alive could perceive him.

Alfred pointed a weak finger towards the window while his eyes remained closed. "Zane, behind you!" Suddenly he snapped awake and blinked several times."Mom, Dad!"

"Okay, son, we're here to take you home."

"Not so fast," the doctor said as he entered the room again. "We need your blood for analysis."

"But why? We have a right to leave here now and so does Alfred," said his mother.

Alfred's dad glared at the nurse holding the readied syringe. "Get me the discharge papers now," he ordered.

Zane wanted to know where this argument would lead but felt urged to do what Alfred had said, to look behind him. And when he did, he saw someone staring back at him with haunted eyes, an old lady – an old lady ghost.

Zane shuddered with fear as the lady hovered slowly towards him, her arms outstretched. "Come, kitty, come to Mommy."

Zane shrunk back, more confused than ever. She can see me, he thought, sort of, but thinks I'm a cat! Then something caught his eye past the old woman, something outside the window that glowed and hovered in the darkness beyond. Zane shuddered again as he realized the Munchers were closing in, maybe not on him, but on the old lady innocently hovering in the ward while an ensuing argument between the doctor and his patient's parents played behind them.

Alfred appeared to be staring in the old lady's direction and Zane wondered if Alfred could also see the light of the Munchers behind the granny ghost.

"Mom, we must go now; I'm scared."

"That's it," his father said firmly, "we're leaving."

"But you can't," protested the doctor.

"We have our rights," Alfred's mother insisted.

Zane tried to figure what was happening with Alfred but felt drawn to the old lady hovering in her nightdress with a ghostly plastic tube hanging loosely from the back of her hand, the other end faded into the air.

"Come, Coco, come pretty pussy," the old lady began to wail, her face turning sad.

Zane froze where he hovered as the lights of the Munchers grew in size and intensity, squeezing out every inch of darkness that could be seen through the window. Then he felt himself shouting at the woman.

"Wake up!" he yelled. But the sound was numb, like his voice was detached from his body. "Wake up, woman!" he yelled again.

For a moment she blinked and looked at him oddly. "Coco?"

"I'm not a cat!" Zane screamed. "Follow me!"

But it was too late; the light of a Muncher burned through the window and began to tear away at the old lady, Zane watching in horror as the woman shrank painfully into the dazzling ball of light, all the time calling out for her cat.

Zane dashed out of the room as another light seeped through the window and began to home in on him. He dived through the floor, past another ward, then down another two floors. He could feel the light behind him closing in. He wanted to catch up with Alfred but knew he had to get away fast. Then he saw it, a furnace in full fire at the back of the hospital. He dived into the fire and hovered amidst the flames. He trembled for a moment and began to feel heat but thought that was ridiculous. His perception of heat abated and he watched through the flames as the Muncher lights leached through the floor above. They hovered around the room and then seeped up through the floor again.

"Dumbo me," Zane said under breath. "Trust me to go to a hospital where people could die. A Muncher's favorite place I'll bet."

He wondered if they had moved on to another soul somewhere and if the old lady had only just died or had died some time ago. He then thought of Alfred and wondered if he had been discharged by now. He slipped his way up through the floors, ever conscious of the local Munchers. He finally spotted Alfred standing beside his parents, clutching his crumpled schoolbag. They were ready to leave and Zane felt relieved and amazed at how his friend could have healed so fast. He waved at Alfred to see if he could spot him, but now Alfred couldn't see him. Zane wondered if one had to be half awake or at the edge of death's domain to see anything unusual like a ghost.

"Alfred," he yelled. But Alfred continued to look at his parents as they left the hospital.

"He won't hear you, boy," said a voice from behind, "But I can hear you jussst fine."

Zane swung about to face a rotund man in clean blue overalls. For a moment he thought the hospital janitor was talking directly to him, but this guy looked neater somehow.

The man scratched a scraggly short beard and leaned in close to examine Zane. "Hmm, not much of a ghost, but you'll do."

"Do for what?" he asked shakily. "Who are you?" Zane floated backwards to look the guy up and down. "You're that dumpster dude, right?"

"Err, Phil's the name," he said.

Zane eyed the man carefully. "Where's Angela? You seen her?"

"Angela? Oh yes, I see. She ain't passed mah way for some time now."

"Well, she was with me in this world but has since disappeared," Zane said suspiciously.

Phil gave a wry smile which dropped quickly. "Maybe the Munchers got her."

"Sure," Zane said. "She knows how to handle them. She probably disappeared down a funnel." He looked down with concerned eyes. "Maybe forever gone from here." He glanced up at this strange dumpster man named Phil. "And why're you here in a hospital? Watching the new dead get zapped by Munchers?"

Phil coughed again and smiled warmly, almost too warmly for Zane's comfort. "You need not concern yerself with them light thangs."

"Why? How?"

"At Vilobino I teach souls like you to cogitate above the sleep curve by exercising the mind, with a little fun thrown in, err ... what ah mean is, by spooking the living wits out of those living folk and learning to resist the *lights* with your mind."

"Vilo... bino?"

"Vilobino, boy, Vilobino... or, as the young call it, Spook School." He spoke the words with intent, his eyes widening with a hint of bloodshot in the corners.

"There you will learn many wonderful ghostly 'n ghastly skills."

"Eh? Like a stinkin' Potter school for wizards?"

"What? Bah! No such hokum, my boy. This is *real* education of an Afterworld you have yet to fully touch upon." He released a puffed-up chuckle. "And you'll scare the wits out of the living; you'll scare 'em to death!"

"Spook people? Like the living will be able to see me? Or stuff I do? How? The living can't see me," he paused, thinking of Alfred, "most of the time anyway."

Phil gripped both of Zane's glowing shoulders and looked him squarely in the eyes, "But you've got the *soul*, boy."

"Hey!" Zane shrunk back and looked at Phil's glowing hands. They felt solid and warm, almost too warm, like living human hands, and almost hot enough to burn into him. "How'd you do that?"

"Touch?" Phil asked wryly. "Here," he said. "See that ol' notice board? I can make the papers move on it. I can rip one off and flip it in the air, and flip someone's mind by the very sight of it," he said with glee.

Zane folded his arms. "Okay then."

Phil walked over to the notice board just as a living human would.

Zane felt a sudden trembling but couldn't understand why.

Phil lifted the bottom corner of a notice sheet pinned to the cork and an old woman sitting nearby watched the paper rise in the air. She shivered and buttoned her overcoat. Phil then ripped the paper sheet off the notice board and it sailed to the floor. He turned to Zane. "See, boy?"

"But how?"

"Look, touch this other sheet on the board."

Zane carefully placed his finger against the paper. A slight electrical sensation rippled through his fingers, but Zane was used to the way he interacted with matter. His finger slipped through the paper and he shrunk back, glaring at Phil. "Doesn't work for me, see?"

"No, you're doon' it all wrong. Where do you get the energy to be angry, afraid and so on? Where do you think you get the energy to fly around the place?"

Zane shrugged. "I dunno."

"Where do you think it comes from?" Phil asked him, his eyes wide with anticipation.

"Beats me."

"My, you is a silly li'l ghost. It is magnetic fields, boy, static energy, solar radiation, vacuum energy and… a thing called Kirlian energy. It's all around us.

It can be drawn from close or afar because we're similar to it. You see, we're like little glows of energy. All you have to do is draw a bit of energy from the paper, the minutest, and then turn it upon itself. Your mind will do the rest. Try again," he urged. "Go on, boy."

Zane held his fingertips close to the paper. After a moment his fingers felt as if they were extending to become part of the paper. He instantly recalled the moment where he was hanging on to the time cube as it flung through the hazy blue void. He could hang on to that grid thing for a while at least. He slowly drew his hand back and the paper followed his fingertips, lifting up into the air before falling flat against the notice board. His face filled with astonishment. "Hey, it works! Can I move anything? Heavy things?"

"The more energy dispensed, the more directly proportional and counter is the reesult," Phil said. "That's why I can't go through walls very well. I am old; my mind is stronger but my energy is weaker. That is why I need assistance to enter other domains."

Zane stood confused for a moment, the confusion abating for the excitement of knowing he could move something in the physical world. He looked up at the strange whiskered man in his clean overalls which appeared loose on him and wondered if the guy had done any kind of messy work at all. He still didn't feel confident enough to trust him but couldn't figure why the stranger would show him all this.

Phil placed hands on hips and gave a slight, narrow smile. "Weel?"

Zane stepped back. Somehow that smile was familiar, those narrow lips and those piercing eyes. This is a funny kind of man.

"Try something bigger," Phil said.

Zane looked around the corridor and noticed a small waiting room nearby. He spotted a book on the coffee table and homed in on it, taking form over the book. He clasped his hands around it but nothing happened.

"No, no," Phil said. "You have to decide first if you want to pick it up or slide it across the table. Sliding takes a little less energy, so try that, but you must decide whether to push it away or pull it towards you. Any effort on matter without intent on direction is futile indeed."

Zane folded his hand over the bottom edge of the book and felt the energy slowly meld with the palm of his hand. He could relate the feeling to being glued to something and he instantly remembered the time when he accidentally Super-glued his thumb to a plastic wing section he had created from a 3D printer at a

Maker Faire, for a model glider he was building. He concentrated hard and pushed against the book and it edged across the table an inch or so. Then he tried to pull his hand away but the book remained glued to his palm. "It's stuck to me. Guess I can pull it back, too."

As the book slid along the coffee table, a nurse nearby stopped for a moment, shuddered and promptly left the room.

"People can't fathom what they don' understand, so they dismiss what they see. It's a limitation of the living."

"Sure, Phil, so how do I let go?"

"You have to remember that you are also a whole, separate being. Only then can you cut off newly-attached energies from your spirit. Release your grip by changing the angle of your hand, like tearing away quickly without a-jerking it back."

Zane tilted his hand sideways and felt a tearing sensation, rather like a band aid lifting from the skin. He drew his hand away to see that it was whole again, not part of the book.

"But how? I have no physical energy. I'm a glowing nothing."

"A glowin' *consciousness*, Zane, that's what you are and that's what allows you to do the things you can do."

"Why can't others do this?"

"Ghosts, you mean? Because they darn well dream," Phil said evenly.

Zane rested against the corridor wall, bewildered by this new information. He felt his spirit tingling with the wall behind and he began to ooze into it.

"Want to be part of the wall?" Phil asked. "You could be part of anything, you know, even living things. If you wanted to, you could settle into that rather nasty looking 'roach up there on the ceiling."

"Why would I want to do that?"

"Some new ghosts *don't have a choice*," Phil said, with a menacing look.

"What?"

"People use reference points in their life. She likes cats. He likes dawgs. She likes bungee jumping and wants to fly like a bird. He's a lowlife attorney and acts like a rat or a roach. Obsessed ones come back as such animals because they are trapped by subconscious dreams."

"Bullshit," said Zane, "Reincarnation?"

"Not in the sense you know."

"Sure."

Phil gave a menacing glare; his face turning red. "So how come there are ver' few ghosts around then, eh, boy? The Munchers don' git all of them, y'know."

Trembling again, Zane floated back against the wall and began to fuse with it again.

"Don' do that; all's fine," said Phil with a strained smile. He rubbed his chin and flakes of powdery skin sprinkled into the air. "You've a lot to learn about all this wretched density. Ghosts who become conscious like you need to escape the Munchers. Some find they can go into lower life forms but will never be able to possess another human body. When they go into lower life forms they lose their memories and intelligences. They become nothing, only to be taken over by the beastly autonomous processes of their host."

Zane gulped. Something about this guy was familiar and that slight Southern accent troubled him.

Phil turned from Zane, an almost rejecting kind of turn that for a moment made Zane feel a little inferior somehow. Yet his trembling increased as he watched this funny-looking dumpster man pace the small hospital waiting room like a live person, not a ghost. Zane could see his footsteps touch the ground and almost hear the steps muffle through the floor. He has presence, Zane mused.

The memory of his heart thumped louder. This guy even had a shadow. But he cannot be seen. Everyone can look right through me, Zane mused, as I'm a ghost, and they can look through him too, but this guy is more than a ghost.

As Zane watched the strange visitor pace the floor, his eye caught a glimpse of colored light spilling out from the man's back pocket. Those colors he had seen before somewhere. A sprinkle of rainbow-colored light lit the area around his back for a moment and Zane stared hard at it. It was then he spotted a shiny metal knob protruding from the edge of the pocket and his heart panicked, as it was the watch he had seen in Harry Abaddon's pocket back in Numan's world.

He felt a gap between heartbeats, like a gap in time with a huge abyss between, a gap ready to swallow him up, steal him away from this afterworld for good. Although this guy looked different, Zane knew now that Harry Abaddon and the Dumpster Man were one and the same.

As he reached the opposing wall, Abaddon swung about and glared at Zane. "You will learn," he said, "to move things about – physical things."

Zane wondered what the hell this guy really wanted of him. He began to think maybe this was his hell that had surreptitiously folded its world around him. He wondered if he'd suddenly wake to see his glowing leg being chewed by a Muncher.

He blinked hard and opened his eyes wide. Abaddon was pacing towards him. He was close now, within a foot of Zane's shivering form. Abaddon raised his arm and Zane ducked from instinct. Dumb, he thought, his hand will just go through me. But then it may not.

Abaddon paused for a moment, holding his arm high in the air before dropping it slightly to scratch the back of his neck. His left eye twitched and he looked at Zane with instant curiosity. "You got the Danbury shakes all 'a sudden. How come, boy?"

Zane thought carefully and hovered down towards the coffee table. "Just dumbstruck by what I can do to matter," he said as calmly as he could.

A slight smile returned to Abaddon's face. "It's just the beginning, boy. But before I can teach you more, you must agree to go to school and learn the ways of the afterworld."

"Can I think about it?"

Abaddon frowned and swung about, pacing away from Zane, his arms behind his back.

Zane had to get away. But he also knew he had to look at the watch again. Maybe I can pluck it from his pocket, he thought. Maybe it's not quite matter like that book, so maybe I can lift it easily and get the hell outta here. That watch is used for something. I gotta have it. He's the stinkin' Devil and, without it, he's gonna be stuffed for sure. But how do I get it?

Zane suddenly felt himself urged to ask: "Why can't you go through walls?"

Abaddon stopped and turned slowly. "I can. It's … just a tad difficult for someone of my years. I told you already. I'm veery old, you see."

"How old?"

"Never mind, boy," he said briskly, "but, having died as an adult, I presume one builds up a load of mental obstacles in one's mind that gets carried 'cross to Death's domain. And the more energy I apply seems to repel me from matter. That energy cannot be diffused so quickly, boy, that's a-why I need the watch."

"Hah. So what you're saying is that all this material manipulation has cost you the ability to slip into matter?"

"I can still do it!" he lashed out, his face turning red and distorted with sudden fury.

Zane shrunk back. "Okay dude, chill!"

"Well chill it is, boy," he said more calmly, his face cooling. "Mah apologies. It… it just takes a lil' more time to sink mah teeth into matter."

Zane hovered back from Abaddon who, embarrassed, tried to compose a feeble smile.

"I'm sure you can do it; you're Phil the Dumpster Dude," Zane said as calmly as he could. He smiled awkwardly and stared into the dark rusty voids that were Mister Abaddon's eyes, eyes almost pupil-less except for a slight sulfur tarnish.

Zane gulped hard and said, "Show me."

A mischievous grin returned to Abaddon's distorted face. He clutched the braces on his overalls, stretched them out and released them. They slapped back against his proud, bowed chest with resounding solidity; however, the more Zane stared at him, the more diffuse this strange devil's appearance became. Abaddon turned and faced the wall, placing one arm slowly into the plaster and brickwork.

Zane could see the tension on Abaddon's crusty face, as if in a kind of gripping pain.

"Now the other arm, and the rest of you," Zane said in a demanding tone. Who am I kidding, he thought, I'm dealing with the stinkin' Devil here, a Southern devil at that, Satan, Beelziwhatshisname, whatever. This guy is one bad dude and I'm telling him to do something. That's wicked! Wait till the guys at school hear this, he thought with rising excitement. But duh, they won't – 'cause I'm stinkin' dead.

Abaddon forced himself against the wall and slowly melded with it. He writhed in an aura of energy that splintered away from him in slices of cold blue light. His whole front was in the wall now, only his back legs and butt protruding.

Zane scratched his head and remembered the sight of Abaddon in Numan's office. He looked so different then and he wondered how Abaddon got rid of his lumpy devil's tail.

"Now you see here, boy, I can still meeld with matter," Abaddon said, his voice muffled through the wall.

"You need to go further."

Zane saw his opportunity and approached cautiously. His hand stole down to Abaddon's back pocket and he stretched out his forefinger to touch the shiny metal protrusion jutting from the edge of the pocket. The metal felt cold, though the light emanating from it gave a burning sensation on the tip of his finger. He probed carefully and felt the chain linked to the watch. He pulled gently and it gave with ease, lifting into his hand.

"How'm doing?" Abaddon asked.

"Just fine," Zane replied nervously. "A little bit more and you'll be in the wall. I'm really impressed!"

He held the watch which felt heavy and he had to look away from its face, which gave multiplicities of flickering colors, causing him to blink rapidly. He covered the watch with his hand and surprisingly, the light barely penetrated it. He tucked it gently in his back pocket and made sure it didn't slip through. It just stayed there snugly which was neat, like it belonged there.

Zane then felt a surge of energy from the wall as Abaddon began to press away from it.

"Wretched density," he cursed, his voice muffled. "But you can beat this, Zane. You have the power to disseminate yourself real easy like," he said reassuringly, "if you want to. You're young..."

Zane's heart pounded with every pseudo, ghostly beat. He had to get out of here fast. "I gotta go," he said hurriedly. "A Muncher's coming. I can see the lights."

Abaddon's arm flung out from the wall, his fingers curling to grope the air. "No… wait!"

Zane watched him probe his back pocket for the watch and heard him curse in a foreign tongue.

Zane swung about and shot away.

Abaddon slowly pushed away from the wall.

Zane glanced behind him and could see Abaddon's head rotate, his eyes glaring down the corridor at him.

269

Abaddon finally released himself from the bind of matter and gasped, bending over and gripping both knees, breathing heavily as if he were truly alive. He stood up and quickly straightened his jacket and probed all his pockets. His face turning red with rage, he gave pursuit.

Zane tried to slip through a wall but felt it repel like a sponge.

"*Boy,*" Abaddon growled, "Come back here."

The words flittered down the corridor but Zane felt Abaddon's voice sounded much closer.

Zane sped faster down the endless winding corridors, bouncing off the walls that buffeted like wind against his face.

"Come back here, you impetuous rascal!" Abaddon now roared.

With a pounding heart that seemed to be one leap ahead of him, Zane whisked his attention back to catch a glimpse of an enraged Abaddon closing in rapidly.

All those neat overalls shredded away from the mock Dumpster Man as Abaddon morphed into the usual travel shape that Zane was accustomed to.

But the pursuing devil shape was different, larger, and now a throbbing red glowing energy mass followed him, picking up speed.

Zane sped forward but felt weighed back by something. He quickly glanced over his shoulder as Abaddon's fiery energy mass closed in. Without looking where he was going, he flung through a wall head on at the end of the corridor, feeling his face stretch back, but finally penetrating the brick to find he had entered another wing of the hospital, which appeared to be an unattended operating theater. He looked at the wall he had just come through. It began to glow as Abaddon's rage tore through the brickwork.

"Why the stink can't I pass easily through walls now?" Zane wondered how Abaddon worked the watch to slip his denser body through walls but there was no time to figure the watch now. He tried to relax his mind as he carefully approached the opposite wall and attempted to fuse himself through it. It felt a little easier this time and with some effort he slipped to the other side. He made his way through the various wards, looking for the shortest, most direct route out of the hospital; he wondered why he couldn't see any windows nearby.

Something tugged him from behind and Zane shrieked aloud and swung about, expecting Abaddon had got hold of him. But it was the strange watch. Zane wondered if its density was slowly becoming part of him. He finally spotted a window and propelled his form ever faster under the rows of fluorescent lights, flinging himself outside to slow down and hover under a street light. He was free. He pressed his mind to move up into the night sky, struggling to gain height as the strange watch weighed him down. He slowly arced high into the air to get his bearings and smiled warmly to himself as he clutched the glowing watch in his hands, amazed at how he could pick up something that felt so tactile. It had solidity, though no one in the living world could see it, but then nobody could see him or the strange devil that called itself Phil the Dumpster Man. Maybe, he thought for a moment before dismissing such an absurd idea, he could make himself solid and visible.

He looked skywards and tucked the watch carefully into his back pocket, and then re-formed into the ghostly ball for speed – but suddenly stopped and concentrated on projecting his own image as a scruffy young dude again. He reached into his pocket and produced the watch. It was still there, and Zane scratched his head, confused at how such a device could change when he did, into light and energy, then change back again. He tucked the watch inside his pocket again and flew off through the night sky towards Alfred's place.

***

"Who calls?" asked Harry Abaddon.

"It's me," said a rough voice, "You left that threshold opening for me to come through, remember? You said he'd be here. Well, I don't see him."

"Oh… it's you. Thought you'd be dreaming by now. Some hope for you, after all," Abaddon grumbled.

"What's wrong?" asked the stranger ghost.

"Darn fool's high-tailed it," Abaddon cursed. He folded his arms and leaned against the wall in the hospital emergency waiting room, observing distraught visitors and the look of anxiety on their faces as they sat and waited for news. He turned and peered through the window beside him and spotted the small glow of Zane's ghost fleeing up into the night sky.

"You scared him away?" the stranger's gruff voice said from behind. "I knew I couldn't trust you."

"The boy is more intuitive than I thought," Abaddon said as he tapped his chin.

"Did you tell him?" the stranger asked.

Abaddon turned to face the scruffy man in tattered clothes, a twisted smile creasing his face. Flakes of chalky powder crumbled and dropped away from his parched jaw, revealing a red leathery skin underneath. His eyes turned to fire for a moment before his face settled to a new shape, a shape twisted with a strange mix of grief and hatred, his visitor thought.

"I told him. He'll come; he has to." Abaddon's eyes narrowed. "We'll help him survive this domain. Now don' you trouble yourself, dear forgotten wretch of a soul."

"I hope so, sir," said the stranger with a hint of distrust in his voice.

"Sir? Oh, nice touch – but please," Abaddon said with a forced smile, "Call me Harry. Are we not on freendly terms? I've given you the ability to achieve density, to be seen by the living, well, for short periods of time at least."

"Yes, sir," the stranger said with a glum look on his dreggy face, a face that had not seen a shower or shaver for some time before his death. His dark blue eyes sagged into depressed sockets of skin and bone, weary from years of struggle, the shadows of defeat casting a heavy weight on his brow.

"You should at least be grateful," Abaddon said harshly.

"Yes sir... Harry," the stranger said nervously, "of course, but my son—"

"Trust me," Abaddon said quietly. "And for now, go back through the doorway I made to your domain until I call. The lights won't git you there."

"But—"

"Go back to your hell, Simon Carter," Abaddon ordered with little care in his eyes.

"What about Zane?"

"He'll come about to my way of thinking." He stopped and folded his arms, nodding to himself. "Though it'll be a might harder now."

"How so?"

"Darn fool took mah watch," Abaddon hissed, "Which puts me on the long route to get back and fetch the other. I'm such a fool."

He rubbed his reddened chin, a chin that appeared to be permanently sunburnt. His eyes narrowed as he glared at the blank wall he had found difficulty merging with.

"And, what's more, he knows who I am."

17: The Sleeper

Angela flew swiftly over the grave stones, unable to spot any of the Carter family graves. She swept up into the sky and nodded to herself that she was lost. Scanning the horizon only told her this was an unfamiliar city. A few ancient-looking churches protruded from a mass of low-rise stone and slate-roofed dwellings that crammed for space on a narrow jut of land surrounded by water on three sides. The sea stretched into the distance beyond. This is an ancient place, she decided, and for a moment she felt perhaps she had slipped back in time. A castle-like dwelling sat behind bleak stone walls in the distance, smeared by low-lying clouds feathering a sandy shoreline, and Angela wondered where she had seen this place before – perhaps in one of her history books. She looked down to the bounds of the cemetery, extensive and almost like a miniature town in itself with small tombs guarded by statues, glaring stone demons and the occasional gargoyle. "I could be anywhere – Italy, Spain, I just don't know." She gripped her face with anxiety and darted around the cemetery looking for a sign – anything in English – but the writing was French and right then she wished she had paid more attention to her language teacher at school. Several people wandered below in groups or alone amongst the graves. They spoke unrecognizable words and Angela scanned the sky for the nearest funnel, wondering if she could ever find a way back to Zane's town.

She relaxed a little and let herself float down slowly, like a feather in the air. A dash of curiosity made her wonder if gravity did have some kind of effect on a spirit, then she dismissed the idea, acknowledging to herself that her mind made her recall the sensation of falling and therefore she did, despite this being a much slower descent. She rested on a large flat surface of marble and assumed her human form as she sat with her head in the hands. A tear tried to emerge but she pushed it back, thinking how ridiculous it would be if she cried because she was lost. She's been lost many times before but, this time, knew she was upset because she actually thought she was heading somewhere for a change, not just anywhere. She stared blankly at the marble headstone before her, weeds filtering through ancient cracks on the tilted stone that had leaned back to rest against the trunk of a huge oak tree.

Angela mumbled the inscription, "Mary Catherine des Granches–"

The granite slab upon which she sat rumbled for a moment and she stood up and looked around quickly, wondering if a tremor had occurred, though the visitors seemed undisturbed. She sat upon the slab again and stopped, feeling a tickle on the edge of her being.

Her heart suddenly leapt; someone was behind her. She swung about to face a pair of tall embroidered boots.

"Pardon."

Aghast, Angela looked up to a man standing on a marble base looking down on her with a heavy frown. He was swathed in what looked like a red velvet cape, his arms folded.

"Ahem..." he coughed. He stood proudly and stroked a short dark beard that narrowly trailed his jaw line.

Angela sprang upright and flicked her hair off her eyes, determined not to display any further evidence of fear. "Where'd you come from?"

"English, I see," croaked the stranger. He quickly looked about the graveyard. "This is not right. I should be in that cathedral." He pointed to a church spire some distance away. "Last time I awoke to notice that is, I was there. But here…" He looked to the slab below him and nodded. "Ah…." He gazed at the other headstones and then looked to the sky. "I see no amis réunis. I have not arrived, and here Englishmen I see have taken France."

"I don't think so," Angela said with slight confusion. Her eyes widened. "Hey, you see me… you're an adult ghost!"

"You're the ghost and you've disturbed my rest," the stranger snapped. "I could feel your presence, your anxiety disquieting."

"I…" She sank back from the imposing spirit. "Who—?"

"I am," he jumped off the marble base, his shoes thudding to the ground with resounding solidity, and he bowed slightly before her, "Monsieur Jacques Cartier, whom," his eyes narrowed while he pulled at his little beard, "appears to have been a prematurely awakened."

"Where am I?"

"You do not know? Why, this is Saint-Malo, France, oui?" He again looked around quickly to confirm his location and nodded, then stroked his beard. "It is true. I have not as yet left this place." He folded his arms. "I must return to the sleep, until the final day. Stand aside."

280

"What?"

He whisked his form towards her and she jumped out of his way. His movements were swift, his seemingly near solid human form sifting into apparition, then back to near solid-looking again, just the way Angela did it, only much faster. He sat on the marble base and began to lean back, his outline beginning to fade. "Now away with you' I must continue my restful slumber."

"No, wait," Angela said quickly. "How come I can talk to you? How come you can stay in this place – an adult ghost – and not be taken?"

Jacques sat up and leaned forward to examine her. "You young and inquisitive, oui? You have a journey, you and others like you. I've had mine."

"But you're still here after…" she paused and took in his appearance. A flamboyant embroidered collar circled his neck, folded over what she could see as a green velvet jacket under the red cloak, "…hundreds of years?"

"Ah, oui, it must be, by looking at you. But I must sleep for the day when I wake. I sleep a purposeful dream that keeps *them* away."

"Them?"

A look of surprise creased his aged face. "Have you not seen them? You mentioned the taking. You know I talk of le force majeure, les Mangeurs."

"Mangeur," Angela said slowly, "I know that word... eat... eating, like Munchers!"

"Munchers? Ah, oui, as you say." He sighed. "These Mangeurs, whatever they're called through the years, they steal the spirits of those gone soft, those whose will power has faded when alive. I learned of many stories from the Huron Indians on my travels through the New World ...ah... when," he tapped his chin, "ah, so long I cannot grasp the numbers without knowing this age."

"Knowing?"

"The passage of time, girl, since my restful voyage begun..." He peered over his nose at her curious glowing face. "What age is this?"

Angela shrugged. "Everywhere I travel the funnels confuse my perception of time, but it'd have to be many hundreds of years after your death."

"Funnels? Conduits, ah yes. A pity," he sighed. "Time catches up to the living. I could have spent the rest of my living days searching for Saguenay, lost city of gold, but war stood in the way, always war. I grew tired of it."

"I know how you feel," Angela said glumly. "Did you fight the Indians?"

"No!" he shook his head vigorously. "Only the Spaniards. Oh, the Indians were affable and tolerant much of the time. When we encountered the Micmac tribe we raised our flag to humble our native hosts, but that is all, per se, to guide our fellow sailors into the New World. They took no real offence at our intrusion but warned us of the soul takers who come in the night to steal the unwary."

"Surely not nearly everyone is taken? Why is it that I cannot see other ghosts, like grown up ghosts? I've only met a few in all my travels."

"You do not listen, petit fantôme. Many specters dream in torment while others rest on reflection of a life fulfilled. Either way the slumber is a barrier to the taking. Was it not your Shakespeare who said, 'we are such stuff as dreams are made on'? I have learned to sleep in peace, from priming in the living world, that is, curiosity, the motivation to explore. But there are stories of the Indians I cannot prove. Many sleep, many are taken and many again are on other planes."

"Planes?"

"Ah you see, the Indians said that ghosts think on different levels and therefore cannot see those ghosts who cogitate on other planes."

Angela thought about his words and her eyes lit up. "Like we are radio waves on different frequencies!"

"I know not these words, but I can see you understand," he said smiling.

A chill suddenly trickled through her entire being as she stood wide-eyed before him.

"What troubles you, ma petite visiteuse?"

"Cartier!" she exclaimed. "Carter?" she looked up at him quizzically. "You must be connected to Zane Carter. You must be related!"

"Perhaps," he said and tapped his chin, tilting his head in reflection. "Do you seek this Zane?'

"Yes! You see I was meant to return to him," she almost tumbled over her excited words, "The Dumpster Man went to direct me to Zane and—"

"Who is this Doompster Man?"

"Someone connected…" she paused.

"Connected to everything… ah yes, please continue."

Angela stopped abruptly and for a moment wondered what on earth she was talking about, but he seemed to understand her even though she couldn't quite understand it herself.

"Anyway," she continued, "I was meant to return to Zane and instead I came here, to you. There is a connection," her eyes lit up, "yes, a family connection. I just came to the wrong person!"

"There is nothing wrong about me," Jacques protested. "I am explorer to the King, I hungered for the reasons why and the lands where." He raised one wild eyebrow and cursed under breath. "But life is no happy ride. There were some early moments where I considered myself as a marionette to the martinets but diligence and observance saw better days." He leaned forward. "Tell me about this Zane personne. Could he be a great grandson and explorer too? Ah, but chance connection not even I could believe, ma amie. It must be…" he raised both eyebrows and looked into her eyes with intent, "…another kind of connection."

"He's … well you must have figured he's dead, about my age." She suddenly grinned. "And we're both explorers of a sort, explorers of the afterlife!"

"Oui, as it is meant to be for the young of this domain. If starved, one needs to explore whether it be inside or out – alive or deceased," Jacques said. "If you alive or if you deceased, you must explore before you can rest, and then who needs to care about the workings of the afterlife? It can look after itself, oui?" He raised a finger and grinned. "Exploration keeps your mind alive. This is the conundrum: many of the mature are set in their ways – they did not use their minds while alive; they did not seek, discover, grasp the elements and ask why. They fell into their own world; inside a lamp of fading light, not seeking what's beyond – they are the ones who build dreams of delusion and despair. If they awaken to conscious afterlife, they are taken. They cannot fight, only run – if they're strong enough and most are not." He sat upright and snapped his fingers. "And les Mangeurs are controlled by the Devil himself, I am sure of this! Despite what the Indians say."

"What do they say?"

"They say le Mangeur is the sun returning to a new day – same sun, different day. To which I add when the Devil fails to snare a soul, there is another chance for him to do so."

"I don't understand," Angela said. "I just want to avoid them."

"Keep alive in death's mind and you shall. The young who, by unfortunate circumstance die, still have an opportunity in the afterlife to explore and become whole without the chains of memories past."

"Come again?"

"Fantômes d'enfants hold the gift an adult loses; that special connection dissipates through the burden of years. Spiritueux d'adulte," he smiled, "– big ghosts – they grow used to the tactile world and therefore find difficulty in learning how to see through the matter of the corporeal while in the afterlife. They are easy prey for ancient fantômes."

"Like devils," Angela said slowly.

"Self-created daemons." Cartier raised his thick eyebrows, his eyes turning to slits as he glared at her.

Angela thought back to Numan's world and the strange devil that took the form of Mister Numan's boss. She still couldn't bring herself to believe it was the Dumpster's Man's brother. "I saw a devil once," she said, "and he took control of others around him."

"Ah, be careful of such demons," Cartier breathed. "They can change shape, beam their energies through to other domains and leave their doorways open."

Angela stared at him incredulously and suddenly recalled what the Dumpster Man said about the watch.

Cartier rolled his eyes and clutched his collar. "Hmm, well, I do not know everything. ma amie. But that's what I've heard … err… picked up on some transient thought from another – oh, I forget where, perhaps a traveling dreamer passing my way. But those doorways, the living cannot see them, and the dead who live in a lucid dream cannot see them either. But doors are there just the same." He sat upright and looked to the sky. "While vivant in the world... alive, did you ever get a feeling about a place? It feels good; it feels bad, hmm?"

"I suppose," Angela said, thinking back to a time when her parents were looking for a new house. Her mother was in favor of one Cape Cod residence that overlooked a playing field and a national park beyond; her father said it gave him the creeps.

"That sort of environ," continued Cartier, "has been visited, the door left open by beings who harbor no good intention. Such doors then allow le Mangeur to pass and seek out souls," he clenched his fist, "and *take* them."

"I see," Angela said, a little distracted. "But they can't travel funnels for some reason. Do you know why?"

"I do not know everything, ma amie, but, in time, we all will know a little more. All I know now is that they can travel funnels if the edges don't touch them."

Angela stood confused and thought about the one that tried to take Zane. Maybe the funnel entrance was too small. She nodded slowly to herself and gazed around the graveyard. "I've never been to France before. This graveyard is elegant. I'm sure the country is beautiful."

"And you can travel without encumbrance, as can our young Zane, oui? And, because you are young, you will be strong enough to fend the life-woven dreams that some adults have manacled to their souls."

He leaned towards her, looking intently into her eyes and spoke softly: "And with all that energy, little fantômes can be noisy, hmm? Noisy little...err... how do Germanics say ... err ... poltergeists?" He brushed his hands in the air and huffed. "Such children unseen and heard I have no time for." He leaned back on the slab.

Angela felt a little offended by that remark but kept her ground. "You want to know more of Zane?"

"In time," he said through a yawn. "We shall meet, all of us one day." He stretched out his arms and sighed heavily. "I must sleep now."

"But—"

"A funnel? Oh yes, take..." he paused, his arm outstretched, and panned the sky. "Take that one. You must have come from that one. It has a soft hole in its side perhaps made by your exit. Surely you can ride its wave to the destination you had intended."

Angela spotted the dark gray funnel wafting towards them. "Okay, mister, but this had better be right."

She knew, however, that there was no other alternative and she waved quickly, spiraling herself up to the funnel hole which was slowly knitting itself together with strings of vapors, closing the opening from whence she came. Without hesitating any further, she dived into the misty tube.

Jacques lay back on the granite slab, folded his arms and smiled to the sky. His form instantly vanished.

***

Angela was thrown about inside the funnel as it thrashed and snaked wildly through the sky.

"Something's wrong!" she yelled to the misty ribbed walls that gave an instant shudder as if to acknowledge her without solution. The funnel heaved again; her progress began to slow and this confused her more as a ghost's ascent into a funnel is supposed to accelerate. A structure blocked her path, a structure within the funnel that appeared to be riding with it. She stared hard as her glowing form slowed and took the shape of her human self. In the abating mists, rows of people reading newspapers and watching small television screens suddenly encircled her and she instantly laughed. "This is an airplane! I'm in an airplane!" She hovered around the cabin, darting between air stewards and passengers dodging trolley carts. She then poked her head through the cabin wall to look outside. The airplane seemed to be flying along the same path as the funnel. A buffeting caused her to fall back into the cabin and she instantly thanked herself for not flying down to see Auntie Chris last summer while alive.

Angela heard a soft bell toll and looked above the passenger seats to see a row of panels illuminate.

"We have entered an area of turbulence," a confident pilot's voice said. "Please return to your seats and fasten your seatbelts."

Angela began to feel sick and wondered how a funnel could buffet her so much, as well as rocking the airplane. If it was the funnel causing the turbulence it could mean that some things unseen by the living could affect the material world after all. Just like the Dumpster Man affecting the muddy soil in his yard. She began to wonder if a ghost school was not so bad an idea. Maybe they can teach her to understand matter and have more control over it or simply how to move physical things.

Somewhere down the end of the airplane a baby wailed. Angela pondered whether her presence affected the plane but instantly dismissed the idea. She poked her head through the exit door. The funnel walls were now pressing against the fuselage. Her heart suddenly jumped. This plane is about to leave the funnel, it's breaking through. It just happened to ride the same course as the funnel for a time, but the two destinations would be different.

"I have to get off!" she screeched.

The fuselage rocked; several trays slid off a trolley cart and clattered in the aisle.

"Oh, darn," someone said aloud.

Angela spotted a man's crotch covered in coffee.

"This buffeting is getting worse; must go now," she said hurriedly to herself.

The plane shook violently, flinging her across the aisle and out through the opposing exit door. The funnel cushioned her and she watched the airplane seep through the funnel wall, amazed at how it seemed to melt the surrounding flutes of cloud. All she could see now was its wing slicing through the misty walls which closed in immediately. The funnel settled and she began to feel the acceleration of her form down the darkening ribbed corridors.

She finally spotted the exit, a green exit, and hoped it would be the lush lawns of the cemetery where Zane's body was buried.

18: Hidden Agendas

Zane hovered low over the tree-lined street where Alfred lived. He patted his pocket every now and then just to be sure the watch was still there. He felt its bulge and relaxed a little. He wondered how it worked and knew that sooner or later he'd find a safe spot and try to figure out the controls.

He approached Alfred's house and hovered down to the front bay window where he could see movement in the living room.

Alfred's parents were arguing over something and Zane couldn't quite hear what they were saying. It sounded like they were speaking another language but the foreign words were broken. Alfred's mom spoke with clicks in her voice and her husband replied with clicks and broken English.

Zane scratched his head and for a moment he felt the solid, dry itchy scalp he was familiar with when alive. Curious, he examined his nails and could actually see flakes of skin, but as he dusted his fingers, the flakes disappeared. He gulped. "Ghosts don't do this sort of thing, surely," he mumbled.

Alfred's dad flung his arms in the air and rattled off more foreign words, intermingled with clicking sounds. His voice seemed strained and almost scratchy through the clicking.

Alfred stumbled into the room in his pajamas. Instantly, Alfred's dad spoke in English, "How are you feeling, son?"

Zane gulped again. "What's with these guys?"

"I feel strangely copacetic, Dad," Alfred said solemnly. "I was always a fast healer as you well know," he looked up into his dad's eyes and frowned as he touched his forehead, "but not this fast. What's happening to me?"

"You're growing up, son. Your body's changing."

"But other kids get injured and take ages to heal. I'm skinny and look weak but heal fast. What's the story?"

His mother looked at her husband with concern and grabbed his arm with both hands. "That incident was a trigger. It's time to tell him, dear. It's time."

More curious than ever, Zane sifted through the glass and floated behind the sofa. He put aside the uncanny feeling of trying to hide. He again looked at his hands which seemed more solid. This is weird. Why am I so solid? Is it the watch? At least they still can't see me.

"I didn't think you were ready for this, Alfred. Sit down, son."

Alfred sank into the sofa, his father sitting before him on the footstool. "We are not from this place, your mother and I," Alfred's father said. "We come from far away."

"That's why you speak funny to each other," Alfred said. He suddenly glared at his mom. "You must be a foreign spy or something!" He stood up quickly and stepped back, stumbling over the corner of the sofa, causing Zane to instinctively flit out of the way.

"You're both spies and you want me to be a spy too!"

"No, dearest," his mother said softly, "not like that—"

"Spies!" Alfred yelled. He bolted for the front door, flung it open and dashed outside.

"Wait!" his father cried.

For a moment Zane didn't know whether to stay or go but Alfred was his friend and he was not about to lose sight of him again. He slipped back outside and felt a slight shock as he passed through the window. It's not supposed to do that, he thought. He spotted Alfred's red pajama pattern down the road and gave chase.

"Zane?" a faint voice cried from nearby. "Zane!" it cried again.

"Angela? Where you been?"

"Trying to find you," she said, catching her breath and stopping herself from wondering how she came to be so short of breath.

"Follow me, Ange. Alfred's in trouble."

Their two glowing orbs darted down the street. Zane could barely make out the pajama-clad Alfred in the night and spotted him entering the park nearby. Alfred plopped onto a park bench and wept.

Zane and Angela approached and Zane gulped, hating to see Alfred crying again.

"What happened to him?" Angela asked.

"Something his parents said. They're strange. It all came about when he was in hospital. His wounds – they healed really fast. The doctor wanted to do tests and all that and—" Zane stopped, trying to gather his thoughts.

"What is it?"

"Well, his parents seem to be foreigners of some kind, or his mother is, anyway. I heard them speaking in a strange language, with clicks in their sentences."

"Clicks? Don't be silly, your afterlife ears are hearing strange things again—" she stopped abruptly, wondering how the Dumpster Man could have put strange poems into Zane's head.

"What?" Zane looked at her suspiciously. "You've seen that Dumpster Man, haven't you. Well, I just saw him at the hospital!"

Angela's face cringed with disbelief. "What? Can't be! If it's him, he sure gets around. Say I gotta tell you about your ancestor."

Zane didn't hear that last comment; his heart raced at the memory of Abaddon chasing him through the hospital. He gripped her arm hard and stared into her eyes.

"Ouch! You're hurting me!" she squealed.

Zane flinched and looked at his hands. They appeared more solid now. "I can't seem to control my density as well as before," he said nervously.

"You look more solid," Angela said. "But I can still see through you, only less so. How'd you do it?"

"Don't quite know," he said slowly. "Look, Angela, that Dumpster Man is no saint. Remember the devil guy we saw in Numan's world? That's the Dumpster Man, the same guy – he just looks different. But they're one and the same."

"No, they're not," Angela blurted. "They're—"

"Then how do you explain this?" He produced the watch he had stolen from Abaddon's pocket.

Angela stared at the watch, a ripple of white streaking across her glossy face. "You have met him!" she screeched. "How'd you get the watch?"

"So, you admit it," Zane breathed.

"No, Zane, not him – Abaddon! Abaddon is the Dumpster Man's *brother*. If he's around here, then we must get out of here now."

"Whaaat?" Now Zane scrunched his face in disbelief. "But Alfred, look at him, poor guy. I'm not leaving him."

"We must, Zane. Abaddon could find us here. I think," she paused, "I think he may even have something to do with the Munchers."

Zane looked away for a moment and then looked at her with concern. "Did the Dumpster dude tell you that?"

"No, but your ancestor talked of them," she said slowly as she tapped her chin, and stared blankly at Alfred who continued to sob on the park bench.

"My what?"

"Well, I think he may be."

Angela proceeded to tell him about the children from Spook School, the graveyard at Saint-Malo, Jacques Cartier and the weird trip back through the airplane in the funnel.

Zane floated, his mouth agape, fascinated by her journey. His eyes wandered to Alfred who sat on the park bench clutching his sides in the cold. Zane shuddered; he was sure he could feel the cold also. He told Angela of the experiment in the hospital and how he could move something; her eyes lit with curiosity.

She touched him on the shoulder and shrank back with a curious look on her face. "The Dumpster Man is a bit solid too and he touched me like this. And I can touch you and you now feel a bit like the Dumpster Man – more solid than just tingling like when I first met you. And he can move things around, material things. I wonder if all that concentration on moving matter has made you more solid in a way, even though the living still cannot see you."

"Yeah, that's what I'm thinking," Zane said, "But I feel a little less solid than a couple of hours ago. Maybe it doesn't last. Somehow I think this watch has something to do with it also."

"Bet he's pissed with you," Angela said. "That's why we must leave now."

"I'm not leaving Alfred," Zane said.

"There you are!" cried a voice in the distance.

"Hey, that's Jake!" Zane breathed.

Alfred sat upright but didn't move as Jake approached him.

"Your mom rang and asked if you were at my place," Jake panted. "What ya doing out here? And in your 'jammies?"

"What did Mom say?" Alfred asked sullenly.

"She's worried about you, buddy."

"She's a spy!" Alfred blurted. "They're both spies."

"C'mon," Jake said, holding out his arm.

Alfred flicked Jake's arm away and Jake shrank back in sudden pain, rubbing his arm. "Hey, how'd you do that? I got a shock!"

"Do what?" Alfred looked away. "You'd better go."

"Did you see that, Ange? Did you see the aura around Alfred's hand when he touched Jake?"

"Yeah, looked like static electricity. You said you thought Alfred could see you earlier. I wonder if it's related."

"Beats me," Zane said, "But ya know it could be nothing but static from his jammies. That Abaddon dude was telling me about different energies. He's so creepy."

Angela tore at her hair, her silvery fingers sliding through the strands. "I used to think life and death was white and black. Now I don't know. Everything is intermingled. Why don't I ever ask the Dumpster Man about these things when I see him? I'm always distracted by something."

"Alfred, come back with me. It's okay," Jake said.

"You all think I'm mad," Alfred sobbed. "Stark raving loony."

"No, buddy, we're just concerned." Jake glanced behind him for a moment and then looked Alfred squarely in the eyes. "Say, guess who I saw this afternoon?"

"Who?"

"Zane's dad!"

"So?" Alfred asked. And then his face lit up slightly, his head tilting slightly. "Here? Where?"

Zane's face flushed to white, all color pushed away from his cheeks as he gawked at Angela and back at Jake. "Yeah, where?"

"I saw this guy. He looked like a bum – you know, tattered clothes and all that. He was bent over Zane's grave. He was crying I think; creepy for him to come back now."

"Too late for Zane," Alfred mumbled.

Angela tried to grip Zane's shoulder as hard as he had touched her and her hand slipped through, but for a slight tingling which raised a glimpse of a smile on Zane's face.

"Your dad's come back," she breathed.

"As Alfred says, a bit late," Zane remarked. "Took my death to drag him back here from God knows where."

"Alfred," cried someone in the distance, "Alfred!"

Alfred swung about and spotted his parents running towards him from across the park grounds. He stood awkwardly, pulling up his sagging pajama pants.

"No, Al," Jake said, grabbing his shoulder.

"Keep away!" Alfred yelled, pushing him aside with an open hand, repelling him backwards to slam into a nearby tree.

Zane and Angela gawked at each other again. "How'd he do that?"

"He seems a little too strong for such a skinny dweeb," Angela said suspiciously.

Alfred suddenly dashed away from them, jumping haphazardly through the shrubs.

Once again Zane felt in a bind, wondering whether to stay near Jake or follow Alfred.

Jake groaned and sat upright, his face scrunched in utter confusion.

Angela looked at Alfred's perturbed face and felt helpless. "Let's go after Alfred; Alfred's parents will see to Jake. He looks okay."

Zane and Angela gave chase down the street, eventually following Alfred into the school grounds near where he was bullied. Alfred wandered past the basketball courts onto the dimly lit sports ground, sloshing his feet into the soft wet soil. He stepped into the change rooms which were often left unlocked and slumped on a padded bench and groaned, closing his eyes from the sharp fluorescent glare of the undiffused lights above. His breathing slowed and he began to slip into a deep sleep, but not before uttering three words: "Thank you, Zane."

"What for, Alfred?" Zane asked as they followed him into the change rooms.

Alfred didn't reply.

"Hello?"

"Forget it, Zane," Angela said. "He's frightened and exhausted. Maybe he knew that we or you were there with him; maybe he didn't. But there's nothing we can do for him."

"It must be almost midnight," Zane said. "I want to stay here with him. I must see what happens next. He was always seen as a bit of a fool at school, always trusting without question and getting trodden on because of it. Now I don't trust his parents either."

"I'm sure it's a misunderstanding. The Munchers, they'll come for sure."

"Maybe not," Zane said. "I have a feeling they won't. Besides I have an even bigger reason for hanging around now – my Dad."

Angela broke into a soft smile, a smile that was reassuring and Zane relaxed a little. "I'm sticking with you this time," she said warmly.

His eyebrows rose with cautious curiosity. "Yeah, what happened back there at the school when we both arrived?"

"Funnel got me while I was not looking," she said. "Thought it was the Dumpster Man but he said it was my spirit's attraction to like-souls."

"Like-souls?"

"Yes, the kids I met at that training town, Spoonville. They're from that Spook School I mentioned, run by a Mister Napes."

"Napes? Another ghost?" Zane asked. "At least I'm hearing of other ghosts, seems most folk get taken."

"Yes, Jacques Cartier confirms what we suspected but he also says people fall into dreams that offer some kind of barrier to the Munchers. Their lives are replayed in a false world because they know nothing else."

Zane looked at her quizzically. "My ancestor, what sort of life did he have?"

Angela proceeded to tell him more of Mister Cartier's stories about the native Indians and the Spaniards and commented that it may have been taught in school at one stage but she probably forgot as her teacher made history lessons seem boring.

Although interested, Zane yawned occasionally as the night progressed and thought that was silly, given the dead don't feel tired.

Angela told him how she slept in the dump yard, a different kind of sleep that also did not attract the Munchers.

"But how?"

"I don't really know," Angela replied. "It was the way I felt when I slept. I felt comforted by something; I don't know what and I felt safe. Must be how Cartier sleeps; as long as he feels safe, he's protected. He says he sleeps for the final day, whatever that is; I forgot to ask, but he sleeps apparently with contentment. Dumpster Man says it's a deeper level of sleep that keeps the Munchers away."

Zane looked down and observed the way Alfred turned in his sleep, groaning occasionally and mumbling something which sounded like 'dinner.'

Angela nodded. "Poor thing hasn't eaten for ages, I bet."

"I miss eating," Zane said. "I miss the taste of food."

"You should try the sensation of eating," Angela said.

"Huh?" he asked, his eyes glinting with curiosity in the harsh light of the change rooms. "You mean that if I can feel a person like Abaddon touch me, then I can also taste? It figures, but how?"

"Shortly after I died, I visited Grandma's house," Angela said. "She seemed happy enough when I got there and I could only guess she had forgotten the impact of my death, her memory going and all that. Anyway, I saw a bowl of fruit on the table and desperately longed for some food, which made me realize I felt hungry and that was weird. So I floated over the fruit bowl and sank my mouth into an apple. It was uncanny. After a moment, I could sense the taste of it and then the other fruits nearby. It was like a fruit salad with banana mixed with apple and orange and peach and pineapple, all in one, all at the same time."

"Because you weren't eating one at a time," Zane said slowly. "Yeah, you sensed all of them at once as your head went through the food. Hey, that's pretty cool. Wish I knew this when I saw all that food at the hospital. Of course, it could all be just our taste memories."

"I'm sure I tasted new combinations," she said. "An', you know, I could also switch off the sense of hunger if I wanted. It was as if there is no more body to tug at my senses saying, 'gimme this', 'gotta have that now' sort of thing, like the alive body was another person with another will all of its own that I no longer have pulling at me."

"Yeah, well, one thing I'm thankful for is not having to go to the you-know-where," Zane said and laughed.

Angela giggled and Zane noticed the brightness her face emitted when she seemed happy. Her smile finally waned as she looked upon Alfred.

As the night rapidly turned to day, Alfred wrestled on the change room bench from what Zane guessed was a disturbing dream, unaware that his parents and others were closing in.

***

A rolling thunderous sky flashed with lightening as Simon Carter stumbled through the dimly lit alley, holding an empty bottle in one hand, the other arm outstretched for balance. He lifted the bottle and sucked the stench of alcohol from it, then flung it to the ground. It didn't break, but skipped down the alley with a hollow clang that caused a few oversized rats to leap out of its way.

A semi-transparent hole burned wider through the stubbly rendered cement wall beside him. It bubbled and tore open like melting film jammed in an old projector, a shimmering light breaking the gloom in the alley. The intense light rippled from white to red before taking form. Abaddon stepped through and smiled, another flash of light glinting on his gold crowns.

"There you are." He cackled. "Dead deluged drunk, whose misery expounds before me."

"Huh?" Simon Carter asked. He scratched his head. "Oh, I remember now. Back already?"

"Not soon enough, I see," Abaddon said as he looked Zane's father up and down. "I see you slipping into your default dream state. Tsk-tsk, there's no hope for the weak," he said with a sigh.

Zane's father belched and pointed at the wall from where Abaddon emerged. "How come I don't see the hole where you come out? It's just a wall."

"Because you *dream*, dimwit," Abaddon said tersely. "It's glossed over by your mind, filled in by your expectations. If you only opened your eyes a li'l', you'd see more, but alas you are a null candidate for the school of thought." He shook his head with dismay. "Why I didn't let you be *taken*, I'll never know."

"I remember you lost your watch," Zane's father said.

"Stolen!" Abaddon hissed. "By your son." He relaxed his composure a little and pulled up his loose-fitting trousers. "I still have the prototype, the one mah dear brother found in the crash of the time cube. How it got there... it's more primitive but it'll serve for now. As for the others, most are in service and some still need to be programmed."

Carter glanced past Abaddon and again could not see the jagged tail he saw draped from Abaddon's backside the first time they had met.

"Looking for my tail?" Abaddon roared. "Do you want to see my horns too?" His eyes narrowed and flashed a glow of sickly yellow light before fading to the usual deep rusty haze.

Zane's father stepped back, tripping over a trash can, watching with dread as several enlarged cockroaches thumped on the ground and scuttled in all directions. They must have been larger than rabbits and he figured he should be used to their size by now; he was thankful no rats had emerged.

"Watch your step, sir," Abaddon said with a wry smile.

Mister Carter, seeing some sense in the subconscious hell he had created for himself turned to Abaddon with a curious look on his face. "Why does everything have to be so exaggerated, big and ugly in my hell?"

"Ah yes, the amplification of material woes is indeed a common characteristic of the dreaming damned," he said with prideful knowledge. "Had I not woken you up to that fact, you'd still be slumped over there in the gutter, your leg being gnawed by a giant rat, over and over again."

"I won't forget, sir," Zane's father said, coughing.

"You better not," Abaddon said tersely. "We have a mission, a mission we couldn't perform a thousand years ago, but now people like your son are waking up, a new consciousness... a new breed of ghost. It's evolution of the dead that allows them to pass on to new awareness, a new enlightenment. They must grow strong to administer the new heaven and to build a wider bridge between the world of the living and the world of the conscious dead."

"Why haven't I passed on to this new awareness?" Zane's father asked, bemused by his surroundings.

"Because you are limited," Abaddon said.

"Like you," Zane's father remarked under his breath.

"What was that?" Abaddon glared at him and then nodded slowly. "Yes," he said and sighed. "They can see better than me, see through all that wretched density and go through it. And unlike both of you, I am too heavy to pass through funnels. We originals need to use contraptions," he said as he dug his hand into his front pocket, "to help break down the very density of death's domains and slip through corporeal matter, to create doorways and so on." He pointed to the cement wall. "Like this."

He produced a small watch which glowed spasmodically, flickering until he thumped the timepiece with his open hand. "Curse its limited range! But it'll suffice till I can get my chronokey back from your son. We haven't a moment to lose," he urged. "Sooner or later he'll work out how to use it."

"What if he funnels away?" Mister Carter quickly looked away, as a slight grin creased his mouth. He didn't want Abaddon to know how proud he was of Zane, of the fact that his own son had a mind of his own in this insane afterworld.

"Oaf!" Abaddon glared at him. "The watch will make him sink through any funnel and then he is open prey to the lights of the night. But if he works out how to use the watch, he could go anywhere through the many worlds already registered in the watch, many more than clocked in this useless prototype." He clutched the pocket watch in his hand and shook it in the air. "I hope, for your sake, Zane's still in his own world back through that doorway, otherwise we're in deep, without being able to get in deep, if you know wha' I mean."

"I know what you mean," Simon Carter said slowly.

"Good, and you are to come with me," Abaddon ordered, "to help convince your son to come to Vilobino."

19: Wonder Fool

"What can we do?" screeched Angela. "I hate bullies."

"Not much," Zane whined.

Josh, a tall and lanky boy stood over Alfred who slumbered awkwardly on the change room bench.

His friend Paul, a shorter, mean-faced, freckled lad grinned from ear to ear and whispered, "What a dweeb. Let's push jammy boy off the bench."

"Nah, wait till Higgins gets here. He'll probably pour toilet water on the fool to wake him up."

"Choice," Paul said and grinned. "Maybe I can back one out in the bucket too."

Zane hovered to the change room door and pushed hard against it.

"What are you doing?" Angela asked.

"Higgins is coming," he panted. "Must shut this door; maybe we can move it and lock it and pull out the key... If I can remember how Abaddon showed me..."

Angela swept to his side. "Even if you do, the other boys in here will be too fast for you and they'll keep the door open."

"Duh me," Zane breathed heavily. "Maybe we can spook 'em. Say, you know sometimes Alfred can hear me when he's half-conscious. Don't know how, but maybe he can hear you too. While I push on this door, can you yell at him to wake up?"

"I'll try," Angela said. She sailed over Alfred and screamed in his ear. "Wake up!"

Alfred swayed his head from left to right, moaning. "Zane's here with his friend."

"What's he saying?" asked Paul.

"Who cares? Make sure the dweeb doesn't wake till Higgins gets here," Josh ordered.

Zane felt his hands seep into the surface of the door as he heard the sloshing footsteps of the approaching Higgins outside. Must time this right, must be precise, he insisted.

The door felt more solid the further Zane's hands melded with the wood. He spotted the approaching fat shadow of Higgins entering the room and pushed hard and at the same time instantly let go of his concentration. The door tore away from him and slammed into Higgins's face, knocking him to the muddy soil.

"Hey!" Higgins screamed, "What you do that for?" He sprang upright, rolling up his fists, and burst through the door. "Was that you, Josh?"

Josh stood agape, staring in the direction of the door. "It just moved on its own!"

"Wind, stupid," Paul said.

"But there was a brick against it!"

Higgins glared at them. "Stand aside," he ordered. "Where's the bucket?"

"Alfred!" Angela and Zane screamed in unison, "Alfred!"

Alfred's eyes suddenly flicked wide open and Paul recoiled with instant fear. Alfred's eyes now appeared bulbous and full of green, fleshy veins. Josh approached with the bucket and stopped, gaping at the glaring green eyes.

"What's wrong with you?" Higgins jerked the bucket from him in a rage, toilet water splashing onto their school uniforms. Higgins didn't care anymore. He already had a back covered in mud from his fall. He approached Alfred as the bucket swayed and sloshed, splashing across his arms. For a moment he froze at the sight of Alfred's puffy green eyes and then blinked, determined not to let his satisfaction of drenching Alfred be swayed by this weird boy. He lifted the bucket and began to tilt it.

Suddenly Alfred sprang upright on the bench and narrowed his green-eyed gaze at Higgins, flinging his open hand out to slam the bucket into Higgins's face.

Higgins fell back against the wall, holding his nose which panged and then he looked down upon his drenched clothes and, finally realizing the contents of the bucket, he screeched, "It's yellow!" He glared at Josh and Paul. "Who did this?"

"It... it was Paul," Josh said, pointing an accusing finger as he took a step back.

"Was not," Paul protested. "Why didn't you see—"

"Let's just get him!" Higgins ordered.

Alfred stood up and stepped back, kicking the heavy bench over with ease as the three bullies closed in.

"You'll pay for this," Higgins yelled.

Alfred flung out his arm and curled back hand, rotating it slightly before striking Higgins with the ball of his hand and full thrust of his arm. He then flicked his left leg up and high to strike another two boys who were thrown back against the metal lockers which clanged and rattled from the force, causing one of the lockers to tip over and crash to the floor.

Zane stared agape at this action and at a shocked Angela. "How's he doing this? Where'd he get the strength?"

"What's that racket in there?" yelled an adult voice from outside.

Angela touched Zane's arm. "The Principal and others – and Alfred's parents."

"Finally," Zane breathed.

The three bullies looked at each other with wide shock in their eyes. They struggled to stand and loped outside, straight into the arms of a teacher and two policemen who held them firmly as they squirmed in the mucky soil.

Alfred's mother hesitantly stepped into the room. Her face seemingly emotionless, she approached Alfred who staggered back into the corner of the room, sulking, his green puffy eyes shrinking back to a streaming burst of tears.

He wiped his eyes quickly and suddenly said something that made Zane and Angela curious.

"Enough of this. It's time for me to go."

It was an adult-sounding voice, not the voice of a quivering school kid who had been bullied too many times. He stood upright and approached his mother and then embraced her.

Alfred's dad placed a gentle hand on his shoulder. "Yes, time to go now, son."

Zane overheard Alfred's mother whisper in her husband's ear, "We cannot return to this place now. People will talk. There'll be questions. Alfred is maturing faster in this place. We must depart."

"It may be too early," Alfred's father replied.

"We have no choice," she said quickly.

"You hear that, Ange?"

"They're really spies?" she asked.

Zane and Angela hovered outside, following Alfred and his parents. Zane spotted a sullen Higgins nearby kicking clumps of soil, head down. The principal was giving quite a lecture, flinging his arms in the air and Angela thought she heard the principal mention the 'expelled' word.

Good, Zane thought. Only problem is if he's expelled he'll go to another school, create another gang and do it all over again.

"Wow, police and all," Angela said. "It's like being alive and a part of it all, all this excitement."

"Well we were part of it, sort of," Zane said. "But we've got plenty in the afterlife to keep us on our toes. Hey, Alfred's folks are leaving. Let's follow."

They darted across the football field and slipped into the back seat of the car where Alfred sat rubbing his eyes as his mother held him. For a moment Zane found it difficult to slip through the car door so he edged his way through the window which seemed easier to pass, while Angela looked on with concern.

"Every time I try to move matter, I feel weighed by it," Zane said. "I can push or pull it and let go of it but it's hard to *pass through it*. It's like Abaddon who has trouble with matter, but I can feel it go again. It's so weird. It may not last but I feel like I'm a bit denser every time I use the skill."

"I heard you were pretty dense," she said with a giggle.

"Funny."

"But serious, maybe Abaddon has lost the ability to throw off density altogether," Angela said. "Maybe the more you use the ability to move stuff the denser you become, like your arm felt when I touched it, and maybe after a while it's irreversible."

"Zane's here," Alfred mumbled as he nodded into a semi-sleep.

"Shhhh and rest, darling," his mother said in dulcet tones. "We're almost home."

"Hi Al," Zane said quietly. "Glad you're alright. Get some sleep now."

Alfred nestled into his mother's side.

"Are we going to show him now?" his father asked.

"The hidden junction? What choice do we have now? I know you don't really want to leave here yet, but Alfred is changing and we can't let this change happen here. It'll be unstable and he may slip out of form," she said.

Angela tilted her head and said, "Form? Do you think they're disguised spies or something?"

"Wonder what they're hiding," Zane said. "Look, we're going down his street so they're heading home. We'll have to stick around to see where they go."

"What about Abaddon? He'll find us, you know."

"I'll deal with him when the time comes. Maybe I should hide the watch."

The car pulled up at their driveway and the double garage door groaned open. Zane and Angela slipped out of the car.

Alfred's father slid his arm past a number of car parts stacked haphazardly on metal shelving, and pressed his open hand against the back wall of the garage. The wall behind his hand glowed softly for a moment. The ground rumbled slightly and a section of shelving began to rise, swinging back and up to meet the ceiling. Some car parts fell over, indicating that the entrance had not been used for some time.

"A secret entrance," Alfred said nervously.

"Surprised you never discovered this," Alfred's mother said in a sweet voice. "You were always most curious about things."

Alfred stepped back.

"It's okay, son," his father said. "This is my second basement. Our special place and it'll be special for you too."

"Not for much longer," his mother remarked. "We'll have to leave everything."

Alfred's dad nodded with concern and ushered them down the dark metal steps into the basement. He flicked a switch to illuminate a small empty room featuring a gray metal bulkhead in the middle of the floor.

Zane thought it looked like a submarine hatch and said, "Pretty neat bomb shelter, Ange. Dad wanted to put one under our house in case the mushrooms came, you know – A-bombs."

"I know," she said with dismissive eyes. "But I'm not sure that's what this is."

Mister Wilson turned the flywheel on the hatch and tugged. A rush of air squealed out from the opening and they climbed down metal rungs into a white room shaped like a cylinder, roughly the size of the double garage above them. Alfred's dad clanged the hatch shut and turned another wheel to secure it. The three stood in the empty room.

Zane scratched his head and couldn't figure out where the light came from as there were no light fixtures, no switches and no controls. Yet light filled the room. "This is a good place to hide from Abaddon," he said.

"Ghosting ourselves deep into the ground may work for a while," Angela replied. She eyed Zane with concern. "Unless you're merging with matter which makes it hard to get back out."

Alfred whimpered and his mother embraced him. "Okay, dear, all is okay."

Angela floated up to the ceiling and poked her head through it. Zane instantly thought of a headless ghost and pushed the thought away.

"Can still go through," Angela said.

"And why couldn't we?" Zane asked.

"Just checking!" She popped back with a smile which dropped instantly and her eyes widened as she pointed downwards. "God, look!"

Zane looked down. The floor where Alfred and his parents stood slowly dissolved into thin air; however, all three remained as if floating in the air. Below, a silver shaft gaped into the distant depths and all three floated down slowly. Zane and Angela followed them down the shaft that stretched deep underground. Alfred's parents held Alfred close to them as they floated to the bottom where a gleaming round metal door awaited.

"How does this work and how do we get back up?" Alfred asked.

"It's a Poddlenov, a gravity reflection beam," Alfred's dad said quietly as the doors rumbled open to a level corridor. "When focused, they work well in narrow confines like this shaft above us. Soon all will be revealed to you about us and where we come from."

"And where you come from too," his mother added.

"They're not spies," Zane said urgently. "More like aliens!"

Angela shrugged and watched the three enter through the double doors. "Suppose I'd believe anything now," she said.

Zane suddenly felt compelled to ask, "Why don't I hear any poems in my head? It's quiet down here. Feel like I should be getting some head talk by now."

"Why ask me?" she said coyly, her face reddening.

"You know something, don't you," he said suspiciously. "You didn't believe me about the strange voices before; now you look like you know something about them."

"I'll explain later," she said quickly.

"You? You're responsible? But how and why?"

"Not me," she said. "Tell you later."

"Tell me *now*."

She huffed. "The Dumpster Man had instilled voices in your head to keep you conscious because you've got a deep-set obsession about your father and you need encouragement to stay awake, with strange words to ponder over, to keep you thinking. Okay?"

"Oh," Zane said slowly. He recalled the fragmented moments of his death and gritted his teeth. He quickly glanced down the illuminated corridor where Alfred's family had passed. "This could be a buried spaceship," he said distractedly.

"Okay," Angela said. "I see you're uncomfortable; that's okay."

"I'm alright, really," Zane remarked, "but when I finally meet that Dumpster dude I'll give him some stink – maybe a piece of poetry, a bad piece to annoy him."

Angela giggled and for a moment she thought she heard her voice resonate on the corridor walls which glowed in different shades of green, the shades pulsating and varying in intensity. A deep green circular door at the end of the level corridor rolled open to one side, the ground rumbling enough for Zane to think it was a heavy door. He nodded to himself upon seeing the thickness of the door, a door like a bank vault had with no handles or barrel locks. Alfred and his parents stepped through to a large domed room of dull green walls, a soft light glowing and shifting from behind. The walls stretched up to meet a high central point where what appeared to be an oversized diamond hung mid-air, glinting as it slowly rotated. Alfred's father pressed his palm against the wall and an oval section surrounding his hand depressed slightly.

A large hole growled opened in the middle of the floor, spilling a soft yellow light which filled the room.

"The way home," Alfred's father said softly. "Where we come from."

"In the earth...?" Alfred asked with a dumbfounded look. "Center of the Earth?"

"Wow!" Zane said, "There's a civilization deep underground in the center of the Earth."

"It'd be too hot," Angela replied. "Unless it's the core."

"Deep down to the center of this planet is not our home, but the way to our home," Alfred's mother said. She brushed her hair aside as she looked down the shaft that glowed all the way to a distant point of blue light. Warm air flowed past them but nothing else and Zane wondered why a lava flow was not erupting right about now.

Angela looked at Zane in awe. "Must concentrate," she said.

"Why?" asked Zane.

"This could be a dream we're in, like we've slipped into a dream."

"Then we'd both be sharing the same dream," Zane remarked. "I don't feel like I'm dreaming."

"That's the problem," Angela said nervously. "It's when we least expect to be dreaming that we're lost."

"But aren't dreams supposed to reflect one's life or obsessions?" Zane asked. "And besides, I don't hear any stinkin' words in my head."

Angela shrugged. "I guess this is real then."

"Where's home exactly?" Alfred asked his father. "How's the center of the earth figure?"

"It's a way to our world, son. Another planet," his father replied. "This place is just a terminus and down through there is the subway, you could call it."

"So how do we get home through here?" Alfred asked nervously. "We'd burn up!"

"Honey," his mother said, crouching down to look him squarely in the eyes. "We use the core energy to transmit ourselves through the skookumchuck to our home planet."

"Skooka—?" Alfred asked, confused.

"Oh that's a funny, appropriate Earth term for riding the rapids," his father said. "Or a wormhole, if you prefer. Think of every planet out there suspended on wires like a mobile or the orbital model in your science class, only a different arrangement with each other. The wires have gravity interconnects. Everything pulls and there is a connection between the planets and the suns they circle, and a connection from that to every other star in the galaxy. We become *transmatter* and use these currents with vacuum field energy to ride almost anywhere. Our world is at sector NQ1, over a hundred and seventy light years away, but we can go back there in a matter of minutes."

Alfred's mother looked down the glowing shaft and pointed. "All we do is jump and our forms are transmitted into an energy that'll travel very fast, finding the shortest route to our home world, just like a neuron in the brain sends and receives commands."

Alfred stepped back. "How?"

"Energy takes many forms," his father said, "and we can rearrange our forms to travel less cumbersomely than humans. Stars and planets are receptors. Try to think of stars as brain cells, each talking to the other, each with its own MAC address, for want of a better description. They're never lonely or really apart. We use them as links to travel. We just focus a bundle of encoded energy into the core which we call unification energy, the same stuff that created

327

the Big Bang, as your Earth teachers inaccurately call it." He smiled at Alfred's astonishment. "When we get home, information will be transmitted to you in the Induction Hall."

"Now I've heard everything," Zane said.

"As we're not coming back, we'll have to seal this bunker from the humans," Alfred's father said. He patted Alfred on the shoulder. "You learned a lot at that school, didn't you?"

"I learned that being different sucks," Alfred sulked.

"You should be happy," his mother remarked. "How many boys get to find out their parents are from another world?"

"Why didn't you tell me until now?" Alfred asked sullenly.

"We had to wait for your maturity, and," his mother smiled with an almost empty, fearful chuckle and said, "it came upon us by surprise, dear. In this world, life passes more quickly but we didn't expect your natural advancement to come just as fast when in an awkward form such as the human body."

"What do I look like then?"

"You will see when we enter our world, dear," she said softly. She made a comment to her husband in the strange language Zane had heard earlier.

328

Alfred paced the domed room and observed his father smoothing an open palm across the jade surface of the dome walls. Portions of the wall pulsed from a green glow wherever he touched them and a rumbling could be heard from deep within the earth. Alfred, Zane and Angela all peered down the glowing shaft which now appeared to move, the shaft walls rotating, first slowly, then faster and faster.

"Maybe another reason for why we get tremors in this city," Zane remarked.

"You didn't tell me it'd spin, Dad," Alfred said. "I feel sick."

"Don't look at it, Alfred," his mother warned.

"Ready yourselves," his father spoke firmly, "cylinder escapement reaching maximum velocity."

All three stood at the precipice, Alfred held between his parents. The whirring rumble of the shaft grew louder.

"Close your eyes," his father said. "I have count." He watched a glowing portion of the domed wall lengthen as a row of tiled lights stretched up to a spinning diamond above. The light changed from a soft glowing yellow to a deeper red and began to flash at the top, causing the diamond to rotate faster. A beam of intense light burst from the diamond into the spinning shaft. At that moment, Alfred's mother and father stepped forward. Alfred stepped back and his father pulled gently. All three jumped into the spinning shaft and Zane and Angela hovered over the hole to watch them fall to a distant burst of fractured blue light.

"What do we do?" Angela asked. "Follow them?"

"We've got Abaddon to worry about back here," he yelled, trying to raise his voice over the drone of the spinning shaft. "Think we can come back?"

"They're not coming back," Angela said.

A drone uttered from above, the lights that had reached the spinning diamond began to draw back and flicker.

Zane quickly looked down the spinning shaft and felt disorientated. He glanced at Angela. "Can Abaddon get through all that rock and dome wall?"

Angela shrugged, looked up and nodded slowly. "It may be slow for him but who can be sure?"

That was enough for Zane. He knew it was now or never. "What the hell," he said as he threw himself into the shaft.

"Bad choice of words, Zane," Angela screamed as she darted in after him.

The two swirled down the spinning shaft, buffeting against the walls. "Hey, this feels rough as," Zane yelled.

"Wish it was soft like a funnel. Why are we rocking all over the place?"

"Don't know, Ange. Try and hold on to me and close your eyes."

They both felt the edges of each other meld in the torrent as they focused on staying together, trailing the disassembled forms of Alfred and his parents. The shaking soon settled and they began to fly more smoothly.

"Hey, we're explorers," Angela said aloud. "Just like Jacques. We can go anywhere, we really can see more than just the world we left behind."

Zane caught her soft smile as they slipped down the conduit and a feeling of warmth smothered him as he looked into her dappled eyes, the green splays of her pupils lighting through all the swirls of yellow and dusky red colors spinning around them and streaking through them. He felt more comfortable now and thought this conduit was now not too different from flying through a funnel, though it was man-made, or alien-made, or whatever Alfred's folks really looked like – he didn't care. He thought of the spinning time cube and wondered if the dematerialization principles were the same and then he thought about how ghosts don't need to dematerialize. And now they were going somewhere fast, away from the world of humans, away from funnels and Munchers and especially away from Harry Abaddon.

End of Book 1

Also available:

**The Chronokey
Book II: Death's End**

www.ingramcontent.com/pod-product-compliance
Lightning Source LLC
Chambersburg PA
CBHW031450260626
47154CB00016B/329